S0-BFC-230

CROW BOY

CROW BOY

MAUREEN BUSH

© Maureen Bush, 2010

All rights reserved. No part of this publication may be reproduced, stored in a retrieval system, or transmitted, in any form or by any means, without the prior written consent of the publisher or a licence from The Canadian Copyright Licensing Agency (Access Copyright). For an Access Copyright licence, visit www.accesscopyright.ca or call toll-free to 1-800-893-5777.

This novel is a work of fiction. Names, characters, places and incidents either are the product of the author's imagination or are used fictitiously. Any resemblance to actual persons, living or dead, is coincidental.

Edited by Laura Peetoom
Cover design by Tania Wolk

Library and Archives Canada Cataloguing in Publication

Bush, Maureen A. (Maureen Averil), 1960-
    Crow boy / Maureen Bush.

(Veil of magic : bk. 2)
ISBN 978-1-55050-429-3

    I. Title. II. Series: Bush, Maureen
A. (Maureen Averil), 1960- . Veil of magic : bk. 2.

PS8603.U825C76 2010   jC813'.6   C2010-900322-5

COTEAU
BOOKS
2517 Victoria Avenue
Regina, Saskatchewan
Canada   S4P 0T2
www.coteaubooks.com

Available in Canada from:
Publishers Group Canada
9050 Shaughnessy Street
Vancouver, British Columbia
Canada   V6P 6E5

Available in the US from:
Orca Book Publishers
www.orcabook.com
1-800-210-5277

10 9 8 7 6 5 4 3 2 1

Coteau Books gratefully acknowledges the financial support of its publishing program by: the Saskatchewan Arts Board, the Canada Council for the Arts, the Government of Canada through the Canada Book Fund, the Government of Saskatchewan through the Creative Economy Entrepreneurial Fund, the Association for the Export of Canadian Books and the City of Regina Arts Commission.

For Mark, Adriene and Lia,
who fill my life with love,
humour and good stories.

CONTENTS

CHAPTER ONE

NOT ENOUGH MAGIC

C AN YOU OPEN THE DOORWAY, JOSH?"
Maddy asked.

"I don't know," I said. I knew there was a doorway here. I could feel it, almost see it, almost reach out with my fingers and touch it. But not quite. I didn't have enough magic.

Maddy and I had hiked to near the top of the trail up the front side of Castle Mountain. We stood at the edge of a small clearing, surrounded by a forest of dark evergreens. Sunlight shone through the branches, and the forest smelled sweet with pine and spruce. A gusting wind tossed the branches of the trees, and crows cawed above us.

Through the trees we could see mountain peaks

across the Bow Valley. The summer had been hot, so there was no snow on the mountains. They looked diminished, somehow, with no snow to outline all the cracks and crags above the tree line.

I could see Mom and Dad below us on the trail, as it switched back and forth up the steep mountainside. Mom had her black hair pulled back in a pony tail, freckles scattered across her cheeks. Dad walked beside her, the bald patch on his head more noticeable from above, their heads close as they talked.

My little sister Maddy stood beside me, her bright blue backpack over her oldest, too-small purple hoodie, too-long new jeans sagging over red runners. Her long blonde hair, lightened by a summer in the sun, was loose and already tangled.

The wind gusted, lifting Maddy's hair and catching the brim of my baseball cap. I tugged it down over my eyes. My hair was just as dark as it always was, my skin just as pale; only my freckles were darker. Even though I was still small, I'd been growing this summer. My favorite blue hoodie was getting tight, and my jeans were too short.

I gazed up at Castle Mountain towering above us. I was shocked at how much like a castle the mountain looked from here, with its row of vertical turrets. I longed to paint it, to capture the light and the shadows, and the fine shadings of colour, but we needed to get through the doorway first.

There's a veil of magic, like a curtain, between the human world and the magic world. It separates our worlds to protect the magic world from humans. Doorways allow magic folk to cross into the human world when they need to.

Maddy and I had learned all about them in July, when a green stone ring she'd picked up in a gift shop turned out to be the magic nexus ring, which helps magic folk cross the veil. Once in the magic world, we had to return the ring to a giant named Keeper because it was too dangerous to use. Ever since, Maddy and I had been plotting to find a way back to the magic world.

It was Maddy's idea to celebrate my twelfth birthday by camping near Castle Mountain. Mom and Dad said there was no way we'd get a campsite in Banff National Park on the Labour Day long weekend, the last weekend before school started. But Maddy begged and pleaded, and Mom and Dad agreed to come up a day early, to make sure we got a site.

So here we were, hiking up Castle Mountain early in the morning, while it was quiet. Maddy and I had raced ahead. We were hoping to find a doorway and slip through before Mom and Dad caught up with us. We knew Keeper, the giant at Castle Mountain, could bring us back to the human world before they noticed we were missing.

After all our planning, our scheming and our convincing, after our long run up the mountainside, we'd actually found a doorway – and I couldn't open it. I growled in frustration.

"What's wrong?" Maddy asked. "You could do it before."

"Once," I muttered. "I opened a doorway once! In July. With the nexus ring to help. I haven't done any magic since then, and I don't feel it as strongly. It's like the magic is still there, inside of me, but really weak. It's not nearly strong enough to open a doorway."

Maddy nodded and glanced down the trail, checking for Mom and Dad. "What now? We don't have much time."

"I know," I snapped. "But I don't have enough magic and you don't have any, so unless someone finds us, I don't know how we can get in."

I sagged in disappointment. We'd so wanted to visit the magic world again, and I ached to learn more magic. The magic that had grown in me in July had faded to just a hint of what it had been.

I thought about how I'd done magic before. I'd used my fingers to draw, to let the magic flow through my art. I shut my eyes, reached out a finger and began drawing on my pant leg, mist and a doorway. No magic. I tried again, struggling to inhale magic, to pull it through my body into my fingers. All I felt was a tingle, not nearly enough to open a doorway.

My eyes snapped open as something heavy landed on my shoulder, sharp claws digging in. It was a crow, perched on my shoulder, staring at me. I stared back, not daring to move. He was totally black – his feathers, his beak, even his gleaming eyes. He cawed, I jumped, and the crow leapt off my shoulder, wings smacking my head.

Maddy stared, open-mouthed, as he flew off, turned and soared straight at me. I yelped and ducked, and he dove, snatching my ball cap off my head. I leapt after him, yelling, while Maddy laughed. Then we both froze as the crow flew to the doorway I'd been struggling to open. A deep patch of mist had filled the space between two trees, with a doorway open in the centre of the mist. The crow flew straight through and vanished.

"Yes," I yelled, punching a fist into the air. Grinning at Maddy, I stepped into the doorway. It was like walking into a thick bank of fog. Mist clung to me, cold and damp and impossible to see through. I felt my way forward until the fog thinned. I stepped out onto Castle Mountain, but I knew I was on the magic side now. And right in front of me stood Keeper.

He was even taller than I'd remembered, twice as tall as my dad, huge and blocky like he was carved out of rock, and grey just like Castle Mountain. Grey clothes, grey hair, grey skin. But he wasn't scary at all, not with that big grin on his face.

"Josh," he said, holding out his hands to me. I grabbed one with both of mine, grinning as my hands were swallowed in his.

Maddy burst through the doorway and Keeper turned to her. "Little Maddy," he said, his gravelly voice full of laughter. He swung her up in a gigantic hug.

The crow sat on a branch, holding my baseball cap in one claw, muttering and pecking at the picture of the blue jay on the front.

"Corvus, give Josh his hat," Keeper said.

The bird cawed and flew past, dropping my cap as he passed overhead. A gust of wind caught the hat and it spun, drifting down the mountain. I raced after it, leaping to catch it. Caws mocked me while I ran.

"You know him?" Maddy asked, watching the crow.

"He is a friend," said Keeper.

"Some friend," I muttered, as I walked back to them, tugging the cap onto my head.

"Crows are friends. Most do not talk to not-crows. So one talks for all. That one is always Corvus. This is Corvus."

We watched him hop along the ground, strutting and muttering. Maddy laughed, but I didn't think he was funny.

"I sent Corvus for you," Keeper said.

"How did you know we were here?" I asked.

"The crows told me," he said.

Corvus cawed.

"Corvus opened the doorway?" Maddy asked.

"Yes," said Keeper, his voice low and rumbly.

"How could he do it so easily?" I asked, as he strutted around us.

Keeper paused to think. "As Corvus, he is all crows. All crows, together, have much magic." He nodded, agreeing with himself.

Corvus kept eyeing my ball cap, intent on the blue jay on the front. After his third fly-by, I snatched it off and stuffed it into my backpack.

Maddy pointed to where the doorway had been, where the mist was slowly dissolving. "Our parents will be there soon. They'll be worried if they don't find us."

Keeper nodded. "Later, I will take you back to them. First, we will visit."

Keeper had brought us back in time once before, so we just nodded.

Maddy and Keeper talked, Keeper leaning down, Maddy looking tiny as she craned her neck to look up at him. I relaxed as I listened to Keeper's deep, deliberate voice. When I first met him, once I had gotten over being really, really scared, I'd wondered if he was slow and stupid. He's not. He just thinks slowly, and speaks thoughtfully.

I turned and looked all around. From this high on Castle Mountain, I could see right across to the mountains on the other side of the Bow Valley. There were fewer clouds here, just scattered white puffs making the blue of the sky more vivid. A brisk west wind pulled at the clouds and kept us cool.

Far below, there was no TransCanada highway running up the valley, no railway line parallel to it, no highway winding past Storm Mountain south to Radium. Sounds were clearer, colours richer, and everything shimmered ever so slightly, radiant with magic. I could feel it seeping into me; I sighed, loving being back.

CHAPTER TWO

IS THE RING SAFE?

C AN WE VISIT YOUR CAVE?" MADDY ASKED. "We didn't get to stay long last time."

"Of course," said Keeper. He leaned down and lifted Maddy up to his shoulder. Then he peered down at me.

"I'll walk," I said, remembering how uncomfortable I'd been high on his shoulder last time.

He headed east, above the tree line just below where the turrets and vertical crevices began, following a narrow path with a steep drop below. He walked slowly but steadily, with long strides in spite of the rough path.

I gazed around as we walked, across the Bow Valley and up at the mountain looming above us. From below, Castle Mountain looked mostly grey. Close up, I could see more colours: dark mustard yellow, muted reds, blue-grey.

Keeper's long strides quickly carried him far ahead of me. I had to run to keep up. Soon I was panting and in pain, but I wasn't going to ask him to carry me. "How far do we have to go?" I gasped.

Keeper glanced back and slowed a little. "The back door is near."

He had a back door into Castle Mountain? I grinned and hurried on.

Corvus flew with us, along with a growing collection of other crows. They surged ahead and then circled back, cawing to each other.

Maddy, Keeper and I talked, too.

"Why did my magic go away when I went home?" I asked.

"Magic weakens in the human world," Keeper said. "It grows in our world. Your magic will grow again."

"Magic doesn't grow in Maddy when she's here."

"Maddy does not need magic," Keeper said.

Maddy looked down at me and grinned.

I made a face at her, but I understood what he meant. Maddy just seemed to fit in here naturally, like she was one of the magic folk, even though she had no magic.

"Josh is the weird one," Maddy said.

Keeper nodded, agreeing. "Josh has a special way with magic."

"I'm glad you sent Corvus to us," I said. "I couldn't open the doorway, not like last time."

"The human world sucks out magic; the magic world builds it." Keeper settled Maddy higher on his shoulder. "First, there was one world, magic and human together. Then humans learned to change the world and magic weakened. The Ancient Ones wove the veil of magic to separate the worlds, to protect magic from humans."

He sighed.

"Now human changes reach into our world, draining our magic. It hurts some magic folk more than others – maybe those who are least like humans. I am not sure. The otter-people are sensitive, especially their babies." His chest rumbled in another deep sigh.

"What's wrong with their babies?" Maddy asked, sounding worried.

I worried too. We'd met some otter-people in July, when Maddy and I had helped rescue an otter-baby trapped in an avalanche. After, they had helped us get the nexus ring back to Keeper.

"When magic is weak and otter-babies get sick or hurt, they are less likely to recover."

"What about Godren?" Maddy asked. He was the otter-baby Maddy and I had helped rescue.

"He was not badly injured. He is fine. But even Godren is not thriving as he should. Otter-babies are usually very healthy."

"Is there anything we can do?" I asked.

Keeper shook his head. "You brought the nexus ring back to me. That is enough."

We walked in silence after that, each of us worrying about otter-babies and magic folk and the magic world.

SOON WE WERE STEPPING INTO A DEEP CRACK in the face of Castle Mountain. Keeper lowered Maddy to the ground, picked up a torch leaning in a corner, and gently blew on it. Immediately flames leapt up. Keeper led us down a tunnel, the torch lighting his way, but his body created such a huge shadow that Maddy and I were mostly walking in the dark. We struggled to keep up, running our hands along the stone walls, stumbling on the uneven ground, until we emerged into a large cave.

I recognized it right away. Keeper had brought us here in July. We hadn't had time to explore it then, and I hadn't seen enough to be able to draw it from memory. Today I was determined to see it all.

The cave was huge and only dimly lit by the torch, but light was coming in from somewhere. I kept looking until I spotted a hole in the centre of the ceiling, tunnelled through glittering rock. Sunlight at the top of the tunnel was reflected through the crystals all the way down, into the cave. The light was slightly amber, soft and warm. When I stood below the light tunnel, staring up at the crystals, I could feel fresh air drifting down, as if somehow the light was pulling air with it.

I walked all around the cave, running my hands over shelves carved into the walls. The shelves were covered in piles of gleaming rocks, scraps of moss of every colour, and bird nests of every size.

Keeper's bed filled a corner of the cave. It was covered in a huge pile of blankets in shades of cream and orange and yellow, topped by an enormous red wool blanket with wide black stripes near each end. A large wooden table sat under the light tunnel, and around it were chairs in a multitude of sizes. A huge stone fireplace filled one wall, and wood was neatly stacked along a second wall, in a pile higher than my head.

While Maddy gently touched the bird nests, I stood near one wall, silently creating a sketch in my head, working out how to manage the deep shadows.

Keeper selected two long branches and knelt by the fireplace. He laid the wood on a bed of coals, and then thrust in the torch. Flames roared and settled as Keeper rocked back on his heels.

"Come and sit by the fire," Keeper said. "Even in summer, a little fire is nice."

It didn't look like a little fire to me – flames filled the fireplace. I couldn't imagine how much fuel it would need, but in all the time we sat there, I never saw

Keeper add more wood.

Keeper pulled up a little willow rocking chair for Maddy, and sat in his own huge rocking chair near the fire. He gestured for me to choose my own. I dragged over an armchair that was just a little too big for me.

I curled up in my chair, remembering the last time Maddy and I had been here, when Keeper had given Maddy a silver ring in exchange for the nexus ring.

Opening doorways in the veil was hard for magic folk. It drained their magic, exhausting them, so they didn't cross very often. The nexus ring made it easy, but it also damaged the veil. Now the ring was safely hidden here in Keeper's cave, so it couldn't do any more harm.

I thought about how many times we'd used the nexus ring to travel between the human world and the magic world, not knowing that each time the ring tore the veil. Now magic was leaking through the tears, lost into a human world that no longer cared about magic.

I started listening to Maddy and Keeper when I heard Maddy ask, "Is the nexus ring safe?"

"Yes," said Keeper in his slow voice. "I am Keeper. I keep it safe."

Maddy leaned forward, an intense look on her face. "Could we see the nexus ring?" She twisted the silver ring around a finger. "Just to make sure?"

Keeper nodded and slowly stood. He blew on the fire and the flames died, as if he'd just put out a candle.

He led us deep into the cave, beyond where I'd

explored, past a workshop filled with tools, all made for big hands but some meant for tiny work. I remembered hearing that Keeper had made the nexus ring.

We continued deep into a corner of the cave to a heavy slab of rock. Setting his shoulder against the rock, Keeper pushed, sliding the slab across the cave floor until he'd exposed a hollow underneath. He reached down and pulled out a worn grey cloth.

Laying the cloth across one huge hand, he gently unwrapped the layers until he'd revealed a collection of rings. I remembered Maddy trying them all on, before choosing the engraved silver band she now wore. I hadn't paid much attention to the individual rings then, but this time we both leaned in, slowly touching each ring, some dark and foreboding, others twinkling with jewels. The nexus ring seemed the least of them, a small jade-green stone ring, plain and dull.

Keeper started to fold the cloth over the rings, but I reached out and stopped him. "Could I look at them a little longer?" I asked. "There's so much magic here."

Keeper nodded. "You feel magic. It will grow again." Then he handed me the cloth. As I sat with it spread across my knees, Maddy slipped her silver ring off her finger.

"Where did my ring come from?" she asked. She held it in her hand, examining the interlocking lines etched into the surface of the silver band.

"Elves made it," Keeper said.

"Elves? Here?" Maddy asked, excited.

Keeper smiled. "No, the ring came from far away. My rings come from many places, many times."

I sat examining each ring. Some I slipped on briefly; others I didn't dare. Finally I picked up the nexus ring and slid it on. It felt good to wear it again. I could feel magic slowly flowing through it into me.

I hadn't noticed before, but the nexus ring had its own magic. When I wore it, I felt more connected to the magic world, and even, ever so faintly, to the human world.

When I mentioned this to Keeper, he nodded. "You are feeling the power of the nexus stone that forms the ring. Nexus means connection, a link. Nexus stone links our worlds. Now we know that it strives to make the connection stronger by tearing the veil."

"Is it safe for me to wear it for a minute?" I asked, feeling nervous.

"Of course," said Keeper. "You will not be opening a doorway in the veil. It is safe to hold."

I relaxed and leaned back against the cave wall. I closed my eyes and became absorbed in feeling the magic world all around me. I could feel the human world too, oddly connected and present, but distant.

I could hear Maddy softly clinking rings as she looked at them. Then she gasped and must have shivered because Keeper asked, "Are you cold?"

"This ring," Maddy said. "It makes me cold."

I opened my eyes to see Maddy putting back a heavily jeweled ring, a cluster of gems surrounding a huge ruby flashing red in the torch light.

"That is the Dragon's Eye," Keeper said. "There are few who would dare to wear it."

Maddy shivered again.

"Come outside and let the sun warm you," Keeper said.

"Can I stay here a little longer, with the nexus ring?" I asked.

Keeper paused as he studied me. Then he nodded slowly, and said, "Bring the ring. You can sit with it outside while Maddy gets warm."

We walked out of the dark cave into bright sunshine, and sat in front of the cave looking down over a lake far below. Maddy sighed as the sun warmed her. We watched brown-coated bighorn sheep on the mountainside across the lake, crows chatting and circling lazily nearby, and a dark bear searching for berries on the far shore.

Maddy and I set our backpacks beside us, and dug out sandwiches and water bottles. Maddy offered to share with Keeper but he just laughed when he saw how small our sandwiches were. He brought out his own – massive buns stuffed with meat.

After I'd eaten I pulled out my sketchpad and drew. The nexus ring got in my way, so I slipped it off and set it on a rock beside me. As I sketched, I felt like I was feeling the mountains, seeing the world through my fingers.

Then I started to tell Keeper about my summer. "I couldn't feel much magic in the human world, but my art was really good. I went to an art camp, and I made a sculpture of you." I felt a little embarrassed, but continued anyway. "It was all carved and angular, and it turned out really well."

Keeper listened carefully. I'd forgotten that about him – he listens with all his attention. I wasn't sure if it was from politeness, or because he had to concentrate to keep up, but it didn't matter. It was great to have an adult really, really listen.

I showed him how I'd made the sculpture, carving clay into all the angles of his face, my arms waving in the air as I recreated the work. When I swung my arm back I hit the nexus ring, spinning it into the air. With a cry I lunged for it, but it slipped past my fingers.

"The ring!" Maddy gasped, leaping up and reaching as the ring spun down the mountain.

"Watch where it lands," boomed Keeper, his eyes following the ring's path.

And then a small crow dove after it. With a throaty, gleeful "ca-ca-caww," it snatched up the ring in its beak and soared away.

CHAPTER THREE

ALEENA

H<small>E IS A YOUNG ONE</small>," K<small>EEPER SAID</small>, <small>SHAKING</small> his head. He stood and called out an order. "Corvus, bring back the ring."

A panicked voice in my head cried out, *The ring – the nexus ring!* I didn't trust Corvus; I had to get it back myself. I took off down the mountainside, scrambling over rocks towards the lake at the base of Castle Mountain. Maddy raced down the slope behind me, struggling to catch up.

Keeper called out after us, "Work with Corvus. I will come if you need me."

The mountainside was littered with rocks. I leapt from one to the next, avoiding the big ones. I slipped, and several bounced down the mountainside, startling a herd of bighorn sheep below me. They bounded away, *baaing* to one another in fright.

I raced on, determined to get the ring back. This was my fault and I had to fix it. Once I'd skidded down the side of the mountain, I ran up the shore of the lake, following the sound of the crows. I glanced back – Maddy was close behind me. Keeper watched from high on the mountain.

Soon I could see crows circling a figure near the head of the lake. I slowed, waiting for Maddy to catch up. Side by side, we followed the shore of the lake to the crows and the still figure.

It was Aleena, standing with the little crow caught tight in her hand.

Maddy gasped, and I felt a shiver of fear.

Aleena was a water spirit. She looked like a tall, thin human woman, but moved more smoothly, like seaweed in water. She stood wrapped in a long cloak and black clothes as tight as skin. Long, loose hair fell past her waist, grey on her head, shading to black at the ends. Her face was pale, her eyes deep blue. I remembered how they danced when she laughed, and turned to black when she was angry.

She'd been nice when we first met, when Gronvald the troll had cornered us to take back the nexus ring. It was only later that we discovered she could be very, very scary when she didn't get what she wanted. And what she had wanted more than anything was the nexus ring.

As we stared at her, she dropped the crow. It fell to the ground with a thud. I gasped as I watched it, willing it to get up, to twitch, to breathe. But it was dead.

When I raised my eyes from the crow to Aleena, she slowly smiled and showed us the back of her hand. The nexus ring gleamed on her finger.

Maddy cried out, "You killed the crow!" and dashed forward. I grabbed her and held her back, afraid of what Aleena might do.

Aleena shrugged. "It's just a crow."

This drove the crows into a frenzy. They circled Aleena, cawing and diving at her. As they attacked, more crows arrived. They flew in from all directions, scolding and dive-bombing Aleena, cawing what I was sure were curses.

Aleena covered her ears, her skin becoming pale and her eyes dark. She turned towards the lake and held out her hands, ignoring the crows as she focused on magic. A spout of water rose from the lake. Aleena drew it higher and higher. When it towered above us, she threw it at the crows.

Water slammed against the flock and flung the crows sideways. Some flew off, squawking and shaking their feathers, while others plunged to the ground. They shook themselves and stood, strutting and muttering. I wondered if there was a way to catch the indignant crows in a painting. But the moment was gone as the crows rose in a cloud, cawing, and launched another attack.

Aleena drew up another spout of water and flung it at the flock. Birds scattered, some squawking in anger, some too stunned to speak.

Corvus cawed out instructions that even I could hear over the noise of squawking. The birds shifted – instead of circling around Aleena, they attacked from the lake side, and slowly drove her back from the water.

Cursing in frustration, Aleena ducked into the forest.

I turned to Keeper, watching us from high on Castle Mountain, and bellowed, "*Keeper!*"

He raised one hand to the sky, and began striding down the mountainside.

Maddy, the crows and I followed Aleena into the forest. We found her holding the ring in her hand, ignoring the circling crows as she concentrated on opening a doorway in the veil of magic.

"Why go through a doorway?" Maddy asked me quietly. "The crows will just follow, and so will we."

I thought about it, and answered slowly. "Maybe she knows there'll be hikers around, so we'll need to look normal for the human world. Magic folk are careful not to be seen by humans. Keeper won't be able to follow, and the crows might settle down. Then she could head to the lake on the human side."

"But if she crosses with the ring, she'll make another tear."

"I know that," I said.

"So what do we do?"

"I don't know," I said, frustration making my voice tight.

"We're responsible," said Maddy. "We brought out the ring."

"I did," I said. "And I dropped it. It's my fault."

"It was an accident, Josh," she said, her voice soft.

"I know, but the damage will be the same. We have to do something." Except I didn't know what to do. I wasn't about to confront Aleena, to try to wrestle the ring out of her hand. She had magic, and she was nasty. "I just don't know *what* to do."

"Well, I do," said Maddy. She marched straight past the crows to Aleena. "You mustn't use the ring to open a doorway in the veil," she said, her voice loud enough to carry over the cawing. "You'll make another tear, and the tears aren't healing as fast as they used to. You mustn't cause any more damage."

Aleena yawned. "Why should I care? It'll heal. It always has, always will. You're fussing over nothing."

Maddy was furious. "Nothing?" she shouted. "The more you weaken the veil, the more human changes will affect your world. And everyone in it, including you. Already the otter-babies are suffering."

"Why should I care about pathetic little otter-babies?"

Maddy looked shocked. I don't think she could imagine anyone not caring about otter-babies.

While Maddy stood speechless, the crows attacked

again. Aleena pulled her cloak over her head as protection from the crows, turned back to the doorway and focused on using the nexus ring to open it, so she wouldn't tire herself by using her own magic.

I watched, thinking frantically. What should I do? Aleena wouldn't give up the ring, and I couldn't take it from her. No matter how angry they were, the crows couldn't either. Keeper might be able to, but she was afraid of him. He would just scare her away, through a doorway or through water. But if *I* could stay with her, maybe something would happen, maybe I could convince her. I nodded, finally sure of myself. I had to stay with her.

Maddy looked ready to speak again, but I held out a hand to stop her. I took a deep breath and bellowed, "Corvus. Stop!" My voice rang with power, like it was projecting magic.

Corvus must have felt it too, because he and all the crows pulled back from their attack, circling higher in the sky, a cawing mass of black.

Maddy gave me a strange look. "How did you do that?"

I just shrugged. I didn't know, and I didn't have time to talk about it.

"Thanks for calling off the crows," said Aleena. "But that won't stop me." She smirked. "You've got some magic there, crow boy. I can see it radiating off you. It's nice, isn't it? Want a little more?"

I swallowed. Oh, yeah, I wanted more. I tried to

focus on the ring. How could we get it from her? "Yes," I said, "I want more magic."

"Josh!" Maddy sounded horrified.

I turned away from her. Aleena needed to see Maddy really angry with me. "Keeper said to just let the magic soak in, but that's too slow. I want more – sooner. Can you teach me?"

She nodded. "You're unusual for a human." She tilted her head to one side as she examined me. "Perhaps I could teach you a little."

I felt a grin forming in spite of myself. "Maybe to water travel?"

"You won't be able to water travel. You're not a water spirit."

"Could you show me, at least?" Anything to stay with her, to stay with the ring.

Maddy elbowed me and muttered, "What are you doing?"

I turned a little away from Aleena and whispered, "I need to stay with her, with the nexus ring. Otherwise, we'll never get it back."

"I'm coming too."

"No. I'll do it. I'm older."

"No way," said Maddy, sounding stubborn.

I sighed. "I'm almost twelve. You just turned eight."

"You might be almost twelve, but someone needs to look after you. I don't trust you on your own. You get weird around magic."

Finally Keeper arrived, his face tight and his eyes angry. He held the dead crow cradled in one hand.

When Aleena saw him, she shuddered and refocused on opening the doorway.

"Stay back," I said, holding up a hand to Keeper. "She's afraid of you." While I spoke my stomach twisted. I knew that Aleena wasn't afraid of us, but Maddy and I were both afraid of her.

I explained to Keeper what we were planning, hoping he'd stop us. After thinking about it for a moment, he nodded and gestured for Corvus to go with us. "Look after them," he told Corvus.

He leaned down to me and tried to lower his voice to a murmur. "I am Keeper. I am responsible. I have failed again. Bring the nexus ring back to me, Josh."

"I will," I promised, although I had no idea if I really could. I reassured myself that at least it was just Aleena. We'd be fine as long as we didn't have to deal with Gronvald the troll, too.

Keeper stepped back, and Maddy and I joined Aleena. Slowly she inhaled and then exhaled. As she exhaled, mist thickened into a dense patch. I could feel Aleena tighten her focus again, and a doorway appeared in the mist. She smiled and opened her eyes. "That's so much easier with the ring," she said, sighing with pleasure.

She stepped into the doorway and paused. "Come or don't come," she said. Then she disappeared into the fog.

Maddy sighed. "Well, the damage is already done. We might as well follow."

So Maddy and I walked forward into the doorway. Mist surrounded us and then was left behind as we stepped into the forest on the human side of the veil.

It didn't feel like coming home. It felt sad and flat, without the vibrancy of the magic world.

Aleena walked to the edge of the forest and scanned the valley for hikers. There were a few on the far side of the lake, heading towards Castle Mountain, but none nearby. She grabbed our hands and pulled us towards the lake.

I groaned. We'd travelled through water with Aleena before – it was amazing, but very wet.

With Maddy and me on either side of her, Aleena tugged us into the lake. Corvus had followed us through the doorway, but he couldn't water travel. Long caws filled the air behind us as we waded into the water.

I gasped at the icy cold, and then shut my mouth with a snap as Aleena pulled us down, deep into the lake. Clinging to her hand, I flowed with the water into darkness, deep under the mountains. I felt squeezed and fluid at the same time, like water under pressure. Then we started to rise, flowing up through cool water, until we emerged in a quiet forest.

CHAPTER FOUR

AT CHINA BEACH

W E SURFACED IN A WIDE STREAM surrounded by huge ferns and gigantic trees. I hadn't been aware of shrinking to water travel, but as soon as air touched our skin, we started to grow. I stretched up higher and higher, Maddy and Aleena growing beside me, until we were normal size again. The trees were still massive, but at least we were taller than the ferns.

We were surrounded by magnificent evergreen trees, enormously tall and huge around. The bark was red and the branches droopy. I recognized them: they were cedar trees, and we were in a rain forest.

Sunlight filtered through the trees in slanting rays, only a few reaching the forest floor. The ground was spongy as we walked on it, soft and moist. The air was cool and fragrant with the scent of cedar. I could almost feel magic here, even though we were in the human world. I could almost see it radiating from the ancient cedar trees. I wondered what it would be like in the magic world.

My eyes followed the vertical lines of the trees, crossed by slanting lines of sunlight. My fingers itched to sketch it. I reached for my backpack and groaned when I remembered I'd left it outside Keeper's cave, my sketchpad on the ground beside it.

I could hear bird song and wind in the branches, and beyond them, the crashing of waves on a beach. Aleena followed the sound to where the trees thinned. We joined her at the edge of the forest.

From there we looked down at a beach stretched thin along the edge of the rain forest. The ocean was huge beyond the sand, reaching out to a horizon marked by a faint line of mountains. Families walked and played on the beach, building sandcastles and collecting seashells.

"I can't go out there," Aleena said. "I don't look human enough. We can't water travel with them watching."

"We could go somewhere more private," I said.

"Exactly," said Aleena, grinning. "We'll cross the veil and play right here, in the magic world."

"No," said Maddy. "We can't take the ring across the veil again!"

Aleena ignored her. "Josh, you open the doorway this time, if you want to water travel. Otherwise, I'll go on my own."

Maddy gritted her teeth. "Josh," she muttered.

"If I can open it without using the ring," I said, "then there won't be any damage."

Maddy sighed.

"I have to try," I said. "We have to stay with her."

Aleena led me to two trees, one leaning slightly towards the other, and said, "There's a doorway here."

I settled myself and drew in magic. It was harder in the human world, but I could do it, now that magic was soaking into me again. I drew softly against my pant leg with one finger, sketching mist and a doorway. As I drew, I could feel energy building; I pulled it into my lungs as I inhaled. When I exhaled, mist blew from my mouth and thickened into a white fog. Slowly a doorway formed in the mist. I felt a thrill of pleasure – I could do magic!

"You did that without the ring?" Aleena asked.

"Yes," I said, smiling.

"But you're not tired?"

"No," I said. "Not tired at all."

"That's strange," muttered Aleena as she stared at me.

I just grinned.

"Yeah, that makes you really special," Maddy grumbled, "Just like a crow!"

Aleena laughed. "My crow boy."

I scowled, and stepped into the doorway. I was immediately surrounded by mist. Slowly I walked through it, until it thinned and I could step out into the magic world.

Maddy and Aleena followed, but I ignored them while I looked around.

The rain forest was older and more powerful here. I could feel magic all around us, radiating from the trees, reverberating in the bird song, and billowing in the ocean waves.

Maddy stared around, a soft smile on her face, enjoying the magic. I could see the magic touch her, not like when it became a part of me, but more like she was a part of it, like she had always belonged.

She played with her ring while she studied the forest, sliding it off and on. As she gazed past the trees to the bits of blue sky showing far above us, she pulled off the ring and used it to frame the sky. A strange look came over her face, like she'd just seen something she didn't understand. Slowly she turned, looking all around the forest through the ring.

"What are you doing?" I asked.

Silently, Maddy handed me the ring. I stared through it and almost dropped it in surprise. I tightened my fingers and looked again. Everything in the forest, every tree, every fern, every fallen leaf, was radiating a luminous light, faint and gleaming. As light was reflected off a tree onto a rock, it was sent on, to another tree, to a patch of moss, on and on and on.

When Keeper had given Maddy the ring, he'd told her, "This ring will help you see magic." Now I understood what he meant!

Aleena grew tired of waiting while we stared at the forest – she wanted to get to the ocean. We climbed down the hill from the forest to the beach of grey sand and dark pebbles, stretching off in both directions along the softly curving coastline. But there was nothing soft about this beach. Even with the tide out, waves roared onto shore with a smash of white foam. Tree trunks were washed up along the highest tide line; the last high tide was marked with shells and seaweed.

To our left the beach curved out of sight. To our right it ended far down the shore at a cliff wall, dark and wet. Huge trees hung down from the slope above the sand.

Finally, I recognized it. "This is China Beach!" I said, shocked.

Aleena grinned. "Very good. That's what humans call it. But you're the only humans here. It's one of my favorite beaches, always a little wild."

"We were here in July," I said to Maddy. "Well, on the human side. When we were visiting Grandma. She lives in Metchosin, near Victoria," I told Aleena. "This is our favorite beach, too."

I turned back to Maddy. "We're on the south end of Vancouver Island, but far enough west to be near open ocean. That's why the waves are so big."

We watched the waves grow as they neared the shore and broke in plumes of white. Then we turned right and headed up the beach, just as we'd done with Mom and Dad, towards the cliff where the beach ended.

"If we go this way, there are tidal pools," I said. "At least in the human world."

Aleena nodded. "Here, too."

The sun was hot as we moved into the curve of beach sheltered by the cliff. At the base of the cliff, a sheet of rock created a ledge that was exposed when the tide was out, and submerged at high tide. All the little pockets in the rocks were filled with saltwater and sea creatures.

Maddy and I walked from one pool to another. We came here every year with Mom and Dad, but we'd never seen so many different creatures. We found red, purple and orange starfish, sea urchins, barnacles, blue mussels almost black in the shade, green sea anemones like flowers in the water, and tiny fish darting in the shadows.

Maddy was leaning over a pool close to the cliff edge when she yelled, "Josh!"

I walked over and knelt beside her.

"Look," she whispered. She pointed into a large pool, filled with nothing but sea anemones. They were larger than I'd ever seen, a forest of tentacles waving in the water.

"Wow," I said. "They're really big."

"No, no. Watch!" she insisted.

So I just watched, trying to figure out what she was seeing. Then I gasped. The anemones were walking around the pool, stopping to touch tentacles with first one anemone and then another, and then moving on again.

"They're having a party!" Maddy giggled.

Aleena joined us and laughed. "Yes, they do like to chat."

Maddy sat down and pulled off her silver ring. She gazed at them through the ring, totally entranced.

Finally, I tapped her shoulder. "Can I have a turn?" I asked.

She smiled and patted the rock beside her. "Sure, but sit down, so if you drop the ring, it won't go far."

I held up the ring and peered through it. Just like Maddy, I was enthralled. As the anemones touched each other, magic flowed through their tentacles, moving from one to another; in each transfer, the energy grew. They weren't just sharing, they were building! Maddy and I took turns with the ring, until the waves crashing on the edge of the ledge started to splash us, and the anemones became quiet.

Maddy and I moved back to the beach and watched the tide come in. I could feel energy surging up from my feet through my body, bursting out of the top of my head. I tried to memorize the details of everything I saw so I could draw it later, but I knew I'd never capture it all.

Aleena played in the ocean, letting the waves break over her. Eventually, she waded over to us. "Time for a firestone?" she asked.

"My own firestone?" I said.

"Josh!" scolded Maddy. "Stay focused."

I quivered, longing to feel the smooth rock in my hand, to draw fire from its veins of gold again.

But this wasn't the time. I had to get the ring back, to keep my promise to Keeper. He trusted me to do this, not to be playing with Aleena. I took a deep breath to settle my mind, and quietly sketched on my leg. What was the best way to get the ring?

Aleena seemed to be enjoying showing us her favorite places and teaching me magic. If we stayed with her long enough, we might figure out how to get the ring from her. In the meantime, I could learn more magic!

I leapt up and followed Aleena to the cliff, dark from water dripping down its face and green with moss. She walked straight into a waterfall pouring down the cliff, into a slight cave behind it. She crouched down, looking at the rocks, and called to me over her shoulder. I couldn't hear her over the sound of the water, but she gestured for me to come. To walk through the waterfall? I tried to ease around it, to not get wet again, until the water hit me, dancing magic across my skin. It was amazing. I stepped right into the waterfall and walked through as slowly as I could.

Aleena gestured to the rocks on the ground behind the waterfall. "See if you can find a firestone."

The firestones I'd seen had been smooth black pebbles with gold threads lacing through them. I looked for shiny black, but because they were wet and in the shadows, all the stones were dark and shiny. Aleena laughed as my hands hovered over the pebbles. Then I let magic seep into my fingers, and I knew exactly where to reach.

My firestone was shining black, with bright gold threads gleaming in it. When I quieted my mind, I could reach in and touch one of those threads. I didn't pull it out – I didn't want to waste any threads – I just needed to know I could still do it.

Aleena nodded her approval and walked back through the waterfall. I followed slowly, holding the firestone in my hand and letting the water dance over my skin again in a play of magic.

CHAPTER FIVE

WATER TRAVEL

ALEENA SET US TO WORK BUILDING A fire. Maddy and I placed rocks in a circle on the sand, above the high tide line. Then Maddy dragged driftwood into a pile, while I collected deadwood from the forest floor above the beach.

Maddy built a base of tiny twigs and dried needles and moss. When she was ready, I held the firestone in my left palm. It was smooth and cool, and I could see glints of gold. I let magic flow into my fingers and danced them across the stone. Then I reached in, caught the end of one thread, and pulled it out of the stone. I dangled it over the kindling, lightly touching down with the tip, and fire flared up the thread. With a gasp I dropped it onto the dry moss. The moss smoked and flared; slowly the fire grew. Contented, I slid the firestone into my pocket.

While we were lighting the fire, Aleena had been collecting food. She washed everything in the waterfall, then laid out an assortment of fish and shellfish on leaves. She set aside a few – I knew she'd be eating hers raw. Carefully she wrapped the others in kelp and laid them on rocks near the flames.

I wasn't sure exactly what she'd collected – mussels rather than sea anemones and starfish, I hoped.

"How can you eat that?" Maddy asked, looking ill.

"What?" asked Aleena.

"We were just playing with them!"

Aleena shrugged. "We have to eat something."

Maddy wouldn't eat any of it. When she was finally too hungry, she nibbled on kelp. It turns out that Maddy likes kelp, salty and crisp from the fire. I hated it – I stuck with mussels and scallops and fish, which were surprisingly good roasted. Still, I felt guilty. I eat meat at home, but eating creatures from a magical world seemed wrong. At least everything we ate gave us so much energy we didn't need a lot.

When we'd finished eating, Maddy washed her hands in the ocean and sat close beside me. "This is hopeless, Josh. She'll never give us the nexus ring."

"What do you want me to do?" I asked. "Hit her over the head with a rock and take it from her?"

"Of course not," said Maddy, but there was a slight

hesitation in her voice. "We've got to think of something. We can't let her keep travelling and taking the ring across the veil."

"As long as I'm opening the doorways, it won't cause any damage."

"Are you sure?" Maddy asked. "No one has ever travelled across the veil with the ring without using it to open the doorway. No one but you could. What if the tears are caused by simply crossing the veil with the ring?"

"They're not," I said. "Keeper said so."

Maddy wasn't convinced. She turned to Aleena dozing on the sand. "You need to give back the nexus ring," she called out, her voice soft but determined.

Aleena rolled over, her back to Maddy.

Maddy raised her voice. "You've caused enough damage to this world. Give back the ring!" Maddy stood, hands on her hips, looking stubborn as only Maddy can.

Aleena didn't say anything, but I could see her body tensing. Suddenly, she rolled and sat up, dark eyes flashing. "Who are you to talk about damaging the magic world, human?" She unfolded herself and stood, hands on her hips, imitating Maddy.

I could see where this was going. If Aleena got mad enough, she'd just leave with the ring, and we'd never be able to catch up with it.

So I interrupted. I walked up to Maddy and slowly

turned her away from Aleena. Then I asked Aleena, "Can you teach me to water travel?"

"No!" she said, shaking off her annoyance in an amused smile.

"Why not?" I asked.

"Because you're not a water spirit," she said with a laugh.

"Yeah," I said, "and I shouldn't be able to open doorways without getting tired, but I can. So could I at least try?"

Aleena nodded ruefully. "Well, you can do those things. You're a strange little human." She shrugged. "We could try."

While Maddy played in the sand, I stripped off most of my clothes, and left them in a pile on the sand.

Together, Aleena and I walked to the edge of the ocean. Aleena took my hand and pulled me down, deep into the water. We became smaller and smaller, slowly becoming part of the ocean.

Once we were water, Aleena let me explore wherever I wanted, but always holding hands so I wouldn't get lost, and never far from the shore and Maddy.

Sometimes I got turned around, not sure where I was, but Aleena always led me back. Fluid and cool, we travelled under rocks and between grains of sand, and flipped into the sky as the foaming crest of waves.

Finally Aleena let go of my hand, to let me explore

on my own for just a moment. I dove down towards the ocean floor, wanting to see what it looked like. Before I could reach it, a current grabbed me and pulled me further out into the ocean.

I struggled, but it was too strong. It pulled me down, deeper and deeper. As I was dragged down, the magic around me changed into something darker and much older. Soon I was surrounded by ancient magic, and lost in it.

Suddenly Aleena grabbed my hand and we rose up and up and up, struggling against the current. The water became clear and the magic normal, at least as normal as magic can be.

Aleena pulled me to shore. I staggered onto the beach and lay shivering while she surrounded me with a blanket of warmth. I felt like waterlogged paper, not good watercolour paper, which is meant to be wet, but cheap stuff, soggy and weak.

Maddy hovered, drying my shaking limbs with my hoodie.

"What were you doing?" Aleena scolded. "If you'd gone any deeper I wouldn't have been able to reach you – you were right on the edge of where I can go."

"How could he do that?" Maddy asked.

Aleena shrugged. "I have no idea. Josh can do strange things," she said, as she stared at me.

It didn't feel at all strange to me. Well, it was strange, of course, and scary, but underneath the strangeness and fear, it felt absolutely natural, like I'd been born to do this.

Maddy was staring, too. "Josh, this is not right."

"What?" I said with a soft smile. "This is awesome."

"No. You're a human boy. This magic is not for you. Not for us."

"You're wrong," I said. "This is totally and completely perfect."

MADDY SAT WITH ME WHILE I RESTED on a log, watching the tide turn as we warmed ourselves in the last sliver of sun. A row of crows joined us, lined up along a tree branch above the beach. They just sat and watched while they quietly muttered to each other. Aleena dozed on the wet sand nearby.

Finally, as the sun set, we leaned down to pull on our runners. When we looked up, Gronvald was standing right in front of us.

The first time we'd seen him, we'd thought he was a short, lumpy man. Once Aleena had cleared away his disguise, we saw him as he was now – a troll. He was short and wide, with rough skin, a lumpy nose, and big ears sticking out from his head. His thick black eyebrows hovered low over his eyes.

Maddy shrieked, backing into me so hard I toppled over the log. I felt sick. I did not want to face him again.

We'd learned before how Gronvald had used the ring to travel between worlds, stealing, hurting and killing, doing anything for more gold. His passion for the ring was even greater than Aleena's, and he cared even less about protecting the magic world.

He leaned toward us, his nose twitching like a dog trying to catch a scent. Then he caught it and stared straight at Aleena, reaching out, his hands opening and closing. He looked totally determined to get the ring back, whatever it cost him.

Maddy had been warm all day but now I could feel her shivering. I pulled her close and swallowed my fear. Even more than getting the ring from Aleena, we had to keep it from Gronvald.

Aleena sidled closer to us, picking up her cloak as an excuse.

"How did he get here?" I whispered.

"He knows all the ways under the earth. Distance doesn't bother him. And the scent of the ring seems to lure him from anywhere."

Gronvald gathered himself in with a deep breath, and then somehow puffed himself up to look even larger and more threatening. "Give me my ring," he said.

"No," I said. "Leave us alone."

"Ah, no," he said. "Not ever. Not in all of time. As long as you have that ring, I shall follow."

A shiver shook me from my ears to my toes. There was no way I wanted this troll following us for all of time.

Gronvald stepped forward, blocking Aleena from the ocean.

Maddy caught my eye and gestured towards a trickle of water flowing across the sand just beyond me. I nodded and took Maddy's hand, while she grabbed Aleena's. I stretched until I could touch a foot to the water, but I couldn't feel it through my runner. I glanced back at Maddy. She mimed falling to her knees – I nodded.

As Gronvald stepped closer to Aleena, she froze, terrified. Maddy and I locked eyes and counted. *One. Two.* On *three*, Maddy yanked Aleena towards her, and I pulled Maddy as I fell to my knees in the stream.

Gronvald laughed. I ignored him while I drew magic up through my body and imagined becoming water. I slipped into the stream, pulling Maddy and Aleena behind me. Gronvald screamed and lunged at Aleena but she shrank under his grasping hands, slipping beyond his reach. I could hear the crows mocking him as we became water.

I took us down the stream into the ocean and stopped, not sure where to go. Once the water soothed her, Aleena took over. Holding our hands, she dove deep into the ocean. Then we travelled inland, squeezing through small spaces between rocks, and flowing under mountains. We travelled for far too long, until finally we started to flow up and I knew we were back in the mountains.

CHAPTER SIX

ENDANGERED SNAILS

THE WATER WAS ICY COLD AS WE ROSE UP between rocks, until suddenly it was as warm as bathwater. We emerged into air and total darkness. I took a deep breath and choked on an overpowering smell of rotten eggs. I gagged and Maddy coughed.

Even once I'd grown to full size, I was standing in water up to my neck. It was too deep for Maddy; she was splashing and choking. I held her so she didn't have to keep swimming.

Aleena sighed from deep in her throat. "Thank you," she said, her voice shaky and low.

"How did he find us?" asked Maddy, sounding very small.

"He wants the nexus ring. He can track it – he'll do anything to get it back." Even in the dark, I could tell Aleena was shuddering. "But he hates water."

Darkness pressed against my eyeballs, so black I lost all sense of direction. I reached out a hand to feel for a wall or bank, and touched something slimy. I yelped and yanked back my hand.

"What is it?" asked Maddy, clinging to me.

I shuddered, and whispered, "Something really slimy."

Aleena laughed. "You guys sound so scared."

"Where are we?" asked Maddy.

"In the human world it's called the Banff Springs cave," she said, sounding proud.

"Banff?" I said, totally confused. "We're in Banff?"

Maddy tapped my shoulder. "Remember, Josh? We toured here last year."

I did remember. The smell was sulphur, and the slime was algae growing around the hot springs. "Why did you bring us *here*?" I asked.

"I love it." Aleena sighed. "The water feels so good."

Good? I waved my hand through the water. It felt kind of like being in a bath – a big, slimy bath. "I can't see a thing," I grumbled.

"Use your firestone," said Aleena, laughing at me.

"Light a fire here?" I asked. "In water?"

"No, silly. Just pull out a thread and use it as a light."

Puzzled, I pulled the firestone out of my pocket and let it drip for a moment. I closed my eyes and drew magic into my hand. I danced it around the firestone, reached in and touched a thread. Slowly I pulled it out; it dangled from my finger, a pale thread of fire. It was a pathetic little worm of light in this huge space.

"Let magic flow through it," Aleena said. I could hear the grin in her voice.

I focused on my hand, and let magic flow through it into the thread. It flared into a blazing torch.

Maddy gasped and hid her eyes.

"Not so bright," said Aleena, an arm across her face.

I pulled the magic back until the light was comfortable, and looked around. The cave was huge, with a massively high ceiling. I could see twinkling through a hole in the roof, far above us. A waterfall splashed down one wall. The falling water was cold, but warm water bubbled up under my feet, the bubbles tickling as they bumped against my legs.

Algae floated on the surface of the water in spotted white mats. I poked at one, and pulled back my finger in disgust.

"Just push it away," Aleena said.

I shuddered and pushed, and it floated away, the surface quivering.

Maddy started exploring the edges of the cave,

where the water was shallower. Aleena lay back, relaxing in the warm water.

I copied her, one hand holding up the firestone light. The water was so buoyant I could float easily. "This is fun," I said to Maddy.

"No," she said. "It's dark and stinky and closed in. I don't like it here, not at all."

I turned to Aleena. "We should go."

Aleena sighed and stood. "Okay, we'll head outside."

She grabbed our hands and before I could fill my lungs or put out the firestone light, Maddy and I were pulled down into the water. We shrank and flowed up a stream of water onto a wet mountainside.

In the moonlight we could see water seeping down a hillside coated in white, with grey algae mats creating a patchwork on top. Aleena helped us walk to firm ground.

The moon was bright and the stars incredibly lively, twinkling back and forth at one another. As I gazed at them, I felt like I could see across the universe. I wanted to linger, to plan a painting in deep blue, but Aleena led us on.

"There's a doorway over here," Aleena said, leading us towards nearby trees. "We'll go to the outdoor pool in the human world."

"We can't," said Maddy, her voice firm.

Aleena just shrugged and faced the doorway.

"I'll do it," I said. I stepped forward and focused on magic while Maddy scowled.

When the doorway was open, Aleena stepped up to it and paused. I could see she was trying to look like she didn't care, but she actually wanted us to come with her. Maddy saw it too.

Did she enjoy showing us around and teaching me magic? Maddy must have thought so, because she said, "We'll only come if you promise to talk about the ring."

I held my breath as I thought, *Oh, Maddy, are you sure? What if she just leaves?*

"Fine," sighed Aleena. "I'll talk about your precious ring."

I let out my breath in a whoosh.

Aleena turned, her cloak swirling, and disappeared through the doorway. Maddy nodded for me to follow.

I slipped into the doorway just as Aleena disappeared in the fog. For a moment, something felt odd. Perhaps I'd been too close to Aleena.

Maddy followed me through the doorway, and behind her flew a crow, large and rumpled, with a flash of white on his wing tips. This was the first crow I'd seen that wasn't all black. With a rough "craw," he flew past us and landed high in a nearby tree.

Bright lights shone on buildings just below us; the town of Banff gleamed further down the mountainside. Near us a tidy wooden walkway followed a stream and circled pools of water.

It was only now that I'd left the magic world that I realized I'd been feeling something new, a special kind of magic. I sketched on my leg as I struggled to figure it out. The feeling had been small, but intense; tightly coiled, a little wild – as it would have to be to exist among sulphur, hot springs and algae mats. It was so strong that when I was quiet and checked for it, I could still feel it, faint but unmistakable, the slightest touch of wildness.

Maddy poked me to pay attention as Aleena pulled us into the stream. We shrank into the flow of hot water and emerged in a warm outdoor pool. As soon as we surfaced, Aleena whispered, "Stay low, and don't say a word."

The pool was surrounded by cliff walls and wooden walkways, backed by a building and wooden fencing. Water bubbled up from the bottom of the pool.

While Maddy and I clung to the edge of the cliff, Aleena wove her hands in the air, drawing steam off the surface of the water, collecting it around herself until she was surrounded by a cloak of fog. Hiding in it, she climbed out of the pool onto the walkway and stepped up to the security camera. "A little water in the wiring usually works," she whispered, as she closed her eyes and touched a finger to the camera.

I braced myself, but all I saw was a quick spark.

Aleena jumped back into the water and called out to us, "Go ahead, have some fun."

Maddy worked her way around the edge, finding shallow places. I waded into the middle of the pool and looked up. There was moonlight here, but it wasn't the same as in the magic world. Somehow it was dimmer, and the stars were less alive.

"We have to talk about the ring," Maddy said.

Aleena frowned at her. "In a minute. In a minute."

Maddy made a face and turned away. I lay back and floated. I liked this pool. It had enough starlight and moonlight to see by, and not too many disgusting algae mats. I could just float, warm and quiet, and watch the stars.

Maddy called out to me, "Josh, look at these." Her nose almost touched an algae mat as she studied it through her ring.

I swam over and took a look. "Those really are gross," I said.

"No, look closely. Here."

She pointed at a little dark spot on the mat. I leaned closer, trying to see in the dim light.

"They're snails," Maddy said.

Those little spots the size of orange seeds were snails? "How do you know?" I asked.

"Because I remember!" she snapped. "These are the Banff Spring snails, and we shouldn't be here!" She turned and climbed out of the pool.

"They're just snails," said Aleena.

"They're an endangered species!" Maddy lectured

from the deck. "In all the world, they only live here! And we're swimming in their home!"

While they argued I studied the snails. I could feel them radiating an energy I recognized. These tiny snails were the source of that tight wild magic, strong enough to feel even here in the human world.

"I can't hurt them," said Aleena. "I'm part of their world."

"Just being in their water hurts them," said Maddy. "But you don't care who you hurt. That baby crow, the snails, tears in the veil of magic. You only care about having fun, about yourself."

Maddy was close to tears. She yanked off her ring and held it out to Aleena. "Look at the snails. Even in the human world you can see that they're magic."

Aleena shook her head, refusing to take the ring. "Yap, yap, yap," she said. Then, at Maddy's scowl, she sighed. "Fine. We'll leave the itty bitty snails alone."

Aleena gestured for me to join Maddy at the edge of the pool. As we climbed out a flock of crows arrived, Corvus at their centre. While the other crows circled, the white-tipped crow cawed to Corvus. The flock landed and strutted around Corvus, cawing to him and listening while he muttered back. Then they flew up in a cloud of black, lined up along the roof of the building by the pool, and began to caw together.

Aleena hissed, "Corvus, be quiet."

He cawed back.

"Corvus, go away!"

But he didn't. They didn't. They just cawed and cawed until the pool echoed with it.

Then a voice boomed, "Hey! What are you doing here?"

I jumped in surprise, my heart pounding.

A man wearing a Parks Canada uniform burst through the gate and raced down the walkway. He slid to a halt as he saw us standing at the edge of the pool, water dripping off our clothes.

"What are you doing?" he asked. "You could be charged $2000 for being in that pool. Each."

I gasped and stepped back. "For what?"

"For disturbing the snails! Disturbing an endangered species is a criminal offence."

He pulled out a notepad and a pencil. "I'll have to call the warden, who will legally charge you. What are your names?" he demanded, staring at Aleena.

Aleena just turned and dove into the water. Fog began to build around her, hiding her as she retreated to the far corner of the pool.

"Hey," shouted the man. "Where did she go?" He shone his flashlight around the pool, trying to see into the fog.

"Aleena, take us with you," I called to her.

She stepped further back as the fog deepened.

"We rescued you from Gronvald!" I cried. "You can't just leave us here!"

The fog was still. The man stepped closer to us.

"Aleena, please!" I said.

The dark figure in the fog moved towards us, the fog flowing with her. A delicate hand reached out, the nexus ring gleaming darkly on one finger. I grabbed Maddy's hand and reached for Aleena's.

She yanked us into the pool and drew us down into the water. As we touched the water we began to shrink. The last thing I saw was the man's stunned face staring as we disappeared into the pool. I laughed as I thought, *How is he going to explain this to the warden?*

CHAPTER SEVEN

STORM MOUNTAIN

ALEENA PULLED US DOWN THROUGH warm water, flowing into smaller and smaller spaces. Then the water became bitterly cold and we squeezed up and up. We arrived in an icy stream in a moonlit meadow.

As I grew I stepped over the rocks to the shore, Maddy beside me. Once I'd reached my full size I was almost dry – only my runners were damp.

I was cold anyway. A sharp wind blew down the mountain behind us. We were surrounded by mountains lit by an almost full moon. A few lights flickered in the valley far below us, and a sheer rock wall towered to our left.

Aleena said, "There was a fire here, years ago." I

could hear the fear of fire in her voice. "It was started by a lightning strike."

I looked down the mountain at tree trunks burnt clean of branches, still standing long after the fire, with new growth surging up from below. In the moonlight it was all in black and white and shades of grey, but I didn't think it would be much different in daylight. To paint it, I'd just need to add deep green for the new growth, and a few spots of colour for late-blooming wildflowers.

The wind gusted and we shivered. "We need to cross the veil back to the magic world," said Aleena. "I can keep you warm there."

"We can't keep taking the ring across the veil," Maddy said, her teeth chattering. "Why won't you listen?"

Aleena sighed. "I'm going to cross, and I'm not leaving the ring here. Not for that troll to sniff out." She walked towards the sheer cliff face.

I squeezed Maddy's hand. "I'll open it," I said. I ran to catch up with Aleena. Drawing magic into my lungs, I exhaled a patch of mist near the base of the cliff.

On the magic side of the veil, the mountains were the same but the slope below us was dark with tall trees. There'd been no devastating fire here.

The wind was just as sharp, though. Maddy shivered.

Aleena said, "If you'd like, we can use the veil to cross time to morning, when it'll be warmer."

"No," Maddy almost shouted. "No," she said, a little more softly. "No more crossing the veil. We can wait for morning." She yawned. "We need to sleep."

We lit a fire, carefully clearing a site on rock, with nothing that could burn nearby. Once it was burning, Maddy and I lay down near the fire. Aleena surrounded us with a blanket of magic to keep us warm while we slept. It was an oddly gentle gesture, for her.

I slept dreaming of failure, of gaping tears in the veil, of Keeper's disappointment, of magic slowly leaking out of the magic world.

WHEN I WOKE AT DAWN, Aleena had fish ready to cook for breakfast, but she asked me to light the fire.

While we ate I realized where we were. I'd sketched near here last summer. Behind us loomed Storm Mountain, partially hidden by deep grey clouds. Below us lay a wide valley, with a river winding through forests. The first of fall's colours showed in flashes of yellow on the river bank.

I knew the highway to Radium followed this valley in the human world; here it seemed darker and more wild. I could feel magic deep in the mountains, and could feel more of it in me, like it had been soaking in while I slept.

"Why did you bring us here?" Maddy asked. I

couldn't tell from her voice if she was just interested, or warming up for another lecture.

"Well, it's not far from the Banff Springs," Aleena said, "and we can walk up to the glacier." She glanced down at me. "Humans call it Stanley Glacier."

A glacier? I thought. Why would she be interested in glaciers? Of course! Glaciers are made of ice – of water – and Aleena loved anything to do with water.

Maddy didn't ask any more questions, but I could see her thinking, planning, trying to figure out how to get the nexus ring back.

As soon as we'd eaten and washed, Aleena was eager to hike up to the glacier. I wanted to linger, to study the colours of the wildflowers in the meadow and to memorize the shape of the mountains. But Aleena was restless, and Maddy and I needed to keep Aleena happy.

I thought about Keeper as we walked, how he felt he'd failed because Aleena had the nexus ring again, how Maddy and I needed to get it back for him. But how? I couldn't see a way.

I could feel magic all around us, in the trees and the milky blue creek and the mountains, each with its own flavour. The creek was light and playful, the trees strong, and the mountains deeply powerful. As we walked I focused on first one magic and then another, getting to know each one.

We followed the creek up a wide valley. Sometimes, as the path twisted, we could see Stanley Glacier gleaming above us. Finally we reached a plateau close to the glacier. The ice looked as if it had poured off the mountain behind it, filling the valley with white. Below the glacier the slopes were covered in small rocks – scree, Aleena called it.

Trees and bushes covered the plateau where we stood, with small purple flowers blooming in patches. A stream wound past, icy with glacial meltwater.

I stared above us at the glacier. It was fascinating, white with shades of blue and grey. It felt alive, almost pulsing. I stood totally still and listened; I could hear creaking. I remembered that glaciers are not unmoving lumps – the ice flows like a river, only very, very slowly. As I watched the glacier I started to feel it, a deep, old magic.

Aleena stood staring, like she was filling herself with it. She smiled softly and turned to us. "This is so beautiful – much better than in the human world."

"What's different?" Maddy asked.

Aleena thought about it. "Well, the magic here is very powerful, and of course the glacier is much larger."

"Why?" I asked.

Maddy shook her head. "Josh, you should remember. Glaciers are melting in the human world. But not here, because of the veil." Maddy looked at Aleena, making sure she didn't miss the point.

Aleena sighed. "They're still melting. Not as quickly, but still melting." She made a face and muttered, "Humans!"

"Not just humans," Maddy snapped. "You're damaging the glaciers, too. As magic leaks out, the glaciers will melt faster. Just like in the human world."

Aleena lowered her head, and sighed. Then she slowly nodded, as if she was beginning to understand. But all she said was, "Let's walk up to the glacier."

I was eager to see the glacier up close, to figure out all the shadings of colour and to absorb the magic, but Maddy stopped me.

"Look," she said, pointing down to the scree. Two furry creatures were wrestling, tumbling across the rocks. "What are they?" she asked.

"Marmots," said Aleena. "Squeaky furballs. They love it up here – those things are all over the place."

Maddy was delighted. She knelt down to watch them.

Aleena sighed. "Can we go? I want to get onto the glacier, not watch furballs tumble over each other."

Maddy was too absorbed to hear her.

"Go ahead," I said to Aleena. "We'll follow in a bit."

As Aleena walked away, I heard cawing. Three crows flew up the valley and landed directly in front of Aleena. One was Corvus. Another was the rumpled white-tipped crow from the Banff Springs. They walked in front of Aleena, scolding with short harsh caws.

I called out, "Corvus, leave her alone." We were just starting to convince her. This was not the time to make her mad.

Corvus cawed to the others. The white-tipped crow

cawed back, head bobbing. Corvus flapped his wings with a long rant of caws, and the white-tipped crow backed off. All three flew to a nearby branch, the white-tipped crow sitting furthest from the others.

Aleena raised her hand to thank me, and walked up the scree slope towards Stanley Glacier.

I turned back to Maddy. She was squatting on the ground, staring intently at the marmots. They were small, furry mammals, like overgrown gophers, silver-grey with dark patches on their heads. Their tails were large and bushy.

I was better at drawing mountains and trees than animals, but I studied the marmots carefully, doing quick sketches on my leg as they played. After a while, Maddy pulled out her ring to watch them. She let me look – the marmots were bright with magic. Then I turned and saw the glacier. It was magnificent, magic flowing as I supposed the ice itself flowed, but cycling back and around, contained and huge.

I could see where the glacier had shrunk and left behind a ridge of small rocks. The marmots scampered all over it as they played. When I looked through Maddy's ring I could see why. It had a magic too, different from the glacier, a little darker and more settled. The marmots were bright sparks of magic against the darker magic of the rocks.

As I watched the marmots and the magic flowing through the glacier, I felt my determination grow. I had to get the nexus ring back to Keeper. Maddy and I had to convince Aleena.

But how? I sketched the marmots to quiet my mind, to let the fear and doubt settle for a moment. As I sketched, my mind stilled, and in the silence came a sureness. *There will be a way. I will get the ring back. I have to stay with Aleena.*

Then Maddy yelped. "Greyfur. Eneirda!"

Startled, I jumped and turned to see Maddy running, arms outstretched. Two otter-people were stepping out of the trees at the edge of the scree slope.

We'd met them in July – Eneirda, who'd taken us over the glaciers of the Continental Divide to return the nexus ring to Keeper; and Greyfur, older and more serious. They looked like small humans, except they were sleek and covered in soft fur, like otters.

Eneirda was about Maddy's height but thinner, with auburn fur and soft tan skin on her hands and face. She watched Maddy with large round eyes, fur in a V down her forehead.

Greyfur was taller than me, with rich brown fur turned to grey on his head and across his shoulders, and amber skin on his face and hands.

Maddy ran to Eneirda, her face lit up in a huge smile. Eneirda smiled a little, and reached out her four long fingers to touch Maddy's.

"I'm so happy to see you," Maddy said. "You made it home safely?"

"Yes." Eneirda smiled, and then sighed. "You did not complete your job, *tss*." Eneirda's voice was low and purry, with a hiss when she was angry.

"We took the ring back."

"*Sssst!* Now you have it again."

"Aleena has it."

"It does not matter who has it. *Sssst!* What matters is the ring tearing the veil."

Maddy hung her head. "I know. We are trying. But Aleena is so determined."

"Aleena is just like humans," Eneirda said.

I flushed. I'd heard her say "humans" like that before, like it was a swear word. "Why are you here?" I asked.

"We are looking for a new home," Greyfur said, his voice deep and somber. "Fire burned our valley. *Sssst!* Usually the veil stops fires in one world or the other. This fire leapt through a tear."

Maddy gasped. "Was anyone hurt?"

"No. We had warning." He nodded his head towards the crows. "But we cannot live there now. We plan to move here. Our babies cannot live near a tear. *Chrrrr*."

Maddy's eyes grew large. "We came through the doorway last night."

"With the nexus ring?" he said, his voice harsh.

"Josh opened the doorway without the ring, but Aleena walked through wearing it. Josh says that won't tear the veil, but we don't know for sure."

Eneirda's mouth tightened and she stepped back from us.

"We're following Aleena," I said, "well, travelling with her. So we can get the ring back."

"*Sssst!* Keeper let Aleena have the ring?" Greyfur asked.

"No, of course not," I said. "It was an accident."

"A crow, a baby crow, grabbed the ring when Josh dropped it," Maddy added.

"I was just wearing it for a little while. Not using it," I said.

"Aleena caught the crow and killed it." Maddy's voice cracked.

"She took the ring and we're trying to get it back. For Keeper."

Greyfur held up a hand to stop us. "Regardless. Aleena has the nexus ring?" His eyes were dark and stern.

"Yes," we both said.

"She must be stopped."

"Yes, yes, we're trying – that's what we're doing – trying to convince her –" we both stammered, interrupting each other.

"*Tss*, you have failed! She must be stopped now!" he snapped.

I swallowed.

"Where is she?" he asked.

I pointed up at the glacier. Aleena stood on the edge

of it, dark against the white ice.

Greyfur strode off, looking determined. Eneirda glanced at us, her face still, and then she turned and followed Greyfur. Maddy and I trailed along behind.

I felt sick. I'd failed to get the ring back. Maybe Greyfur and Eneirda could, but if they failed, too, and made Aleena angry enough, she'd just leave. Then we'd never get it back. Never!

CHAPTER EIGHT

THROUGH THE RING

G REYFUR STRODE UP THE LOOSE ROCKS TO the base of the glacier. "Aleena!" he growled. "You damage our world. *Sssst!* You must give back the nexus ring."

We raced after him, sliding on the scree.

Aleena turned to him, her face cold and pale as the glacier, her eyes reflecting the blue in the shadows. "I do what I want," she said.

"Regardless of the consequences?"

"I am not concerned with *consequences!*" She spat it out like it was a swear word.

"*Tss.* Then you are no better than a *human,*" Greyfur spat back, like he was using a swear word, too.

Maddy slipped her hand into mine. I glanced down –

her face was as pale as Aleena's.

The crows gathered, congregating on the rocks in a mass of black, silent for once. Corvus watched from above, perched on a branch.

Greyfur stepped closer. "*Sssst!* You must not use the ring!"

Aleena peered down her nose at him, "And who exactly is going to stop me?"

Greyfur stepped up to Aleena, shoulders square. "I will stop you."

Aleena laughed.

Eneirda joined him. "And I will stop you. *Tss.*"

Aleena shrugged.

Then Maddy slipped her hand out of mine and stood on Eneirda's other side. They made a strange picture, Aleena tall and thin, her dark cloak swirling in the wind; Greyfur, Maddy and Eneirda all so small, clustered in front of her, trying to look intimidating.

I stepped forward. Even though I didn't want to make Aleena mad, I couldn't let Maddy stand there without me.

The crows joined me, first Corvus and the white-tipped crow, and then the rest of the flock, all walking forward, facing Aleena in silence.

She just laughed. "Even with all of you together, do you really think you can stop me?"

The crows surged forward in a cawing mass, but Greyfur held out a hand to stop them. "We do not wish to harm you."

The crows cawed in disagreement.

"We do not wish to harm you," he repeated, frowning down at the crows. "But we will not allow you to harm the veil. *Sssst!* You must give back the nexus ring!"

Aleena spun around and strode onto the glacier. Then she turned. "Just try and stop me," she said.

The white-tipped crow rushed at Aleena, squawking, wings flapping, jabbing his beak as he scolded her.

Her lips moving silently, Aleena reached out, floated a chunk of ice off the face of the glacier and flung it at the crow.

He squawked and leapt away, but the ice caught him across the side of the head and he fell to the ground.

The crows dove at Aleena, pecking at her head and yanking her hair. The white-tipped crow cheered them on as he struggled to his feet.

Aleena reached up to the grey clouds huddled around the peak of Storm Mountain and drew them to her. They moved slowly at first, and then faster and faster as if they couldn't wait to reach her. They boiled overhead, dark as night.

Then hail plummeted from the sky, hard balls of ice smashing into everything – Maddy and me, the otter-people, the crows. We cried out and raised our hands to protect our heads. Leaves were stripped off the trees, filling the air with the scent of crushed plants.

Hail smacked my head and shoulders, hard and icy, leaving welts and bruises. Maddy cried out and touched a hand to the side of her head. When she pulled it away, it was red with blood.

Aleena stood in the centre of the fury, perfectly dry, not touched by a single hail stone. She looked exultant, all her focus on her hands, bringing down destruction.

As the otter-people and the crows closed in around her, I could see her planning her escape. If she left, I wouldn't be able to follow her. I could water travel, but I wasn't a tracker. We'd never find her.

I stared at the otter-people, Maddy, and the crows, all furious, battered and determined. Several crows lay unmoving on the ground. Eneirda and Greyfur both had bruises on their foreheads and bloody patches across their shoulders. Maddy held a hand to her head, trying to stop the bleeding. Aleena looked prepared to fight forever.

I stepped into the middle of the crowd, held out my arms and cried, "Stop!" Magic reverberated in my voice.

Everyone turned to me, suddenly silent.

"We have to stop," I said. "You have to let Maddy and me take care of this. We will get the nexus ring back. We will protect the magic world."

They stared at me in stunned silence.

Then the white-tipped crow spat out a single, scornful, "Cawww!"

Eneirda muttered, "Humans," and Greyfur frowned.

"Keeper trusts us," I said. "Maddy and I will find a way. If we keep fighting, more of us will be hurt." I nodded to the crows. "Aleena will leave. We will never get the ring back."

I could see Maddy torn between my logic and her own determination to fight. She stared into my eyes, took a deep breath and nodded. She stepped to my side. "I agree," she said.

Greyfur and Eneirda hissed. Greyfur opened his mouth to speak, but I stared him down, feeling totally determined and sure. He stopped, gave one slow nod and stepped back. "You must succeed," he said. "*Tss*, you must get the ring back to Keeper."

"I will," I said.

I turned to Aleena. "Come with us, please," I said. I watched her face as I spoke. Underneath the fury flashing in her eyes I could see a hint of hurt and fear. I reached out a hand to her. She sighed and nodded, and the anger drained from her face.

As we turned to leave, Maddy said, "I'll just be a moment." I headed down the scree slope with Aleena as Maddy asked Eneirda, "What will you do now?"

"We will continue looking for a safe home. We will go far away from where you have been, far from where you might be."

I felt sick, and more determined than ever to stop this.

WE WALKED BACK TO WHERE we'd spent the night, near the creek by the base of the cliff face. Clouds from the storm followed us, as if they wanted to be close to Aleena.

Maddy's head finally stopped bleeding; I helped her wash the blood out of her hair.

The crows settled nearby, checking each other's injuries and splashing in the creek. The white-tipped crow paced and bossed, while Corvus sat back and groomed his feathers.

Maddy watched them through her silver ring, and then leaned back. She smiled and rocked slightly as she looked across the valley to the far mountains, enjoying seeing magic so clearly. Then she turned to study the rock face behind us. Her body stiffened as she stared through the ring. "Josh," she said quietly, sounding puzzled.

"Hmmm?" I said.

"Come look at this." Now her voice sounded more urgent as she waved a hand at me.

I sat beside her, and as she handed me the ring, she gave me a look filled with pity, like she knew that what I was going to see would break my heart. Not understanding, I took the ring and peered through it.

I could see magic, like the radiance that shimmered

in everything I saw in the magic world, but it was more substantial through the ring, like it was an actual thing hovering in the air, light and beautiful. The trees each had their own radiance, their own presence, as if you could walk up to a spruce tree and have a conversation.

Corvus and his crows circled us and cawed, but this time I didn't mind. They were magnificent. When Corvus flew, magic stretched from his wingtips across the sky.

Then I saw the doorway, near the face of the rock wall that rose high above us. It was closed, but the edges pulsed with magic. Surrounding it was the veil, translucent white as if woven of the finest gossamer threads, like spider's silk. And stretching out from the doorway was a great long gash in the veil.

My heart stopped. Maddy was right! Magic was pouring through the tear like water through a hole in a dam, except this was golden and radiant. I longed to reach out and pull the tear closed, to use my hands to fill the gap, to stop that leak.

Aleena wandered over, asking why we were so quiet. Suddenly, I knew exactly what to do. Without saying a word, I handed her Maddy's ring and pointed at the doorway. She stared through the ring and gasped. As the colour drained from her face, she closed her eyes, unable to look. Silently, she handed the ring back and walked away. I had no idea what she was thinking, but I knew that we were getting close.

Later, I watched her staring across the valley, the nexus ring in the palm of her hand, her fingers closing over it and opening again as if she couldn't decide if she should keep it or let it go.

Then Maddy screamed. Aleena and I both spun around. Maddy stood by the creek, her whole body tight as she pointed to the doorway at the base of the rock face.

As we stared, a hand appeared, large and dirty, with thick, stubby fingers. It groped in the air, struggling to grab something.

"Give me your ring," I whispered to Maddy. I peered through the silver ring and watched, stunned. The hand reached through the tear, grabbed an edge of the veil and pulled the tear wider. Then Gronvald stepped through, without ever opening the doorway itself, full of energy and delighted with his new trick.

He stared at us, sniffing. When he caught the scent of the nexus ring, his left hand reached out, twitching. Slowly, his hand opened and closed, and then opened again – just like Aleena's, grasping, longing for the ring.

Grinning, his hands reaching, Gronvald moved from the doorway, placing himself between Aleena and the stream.

I glanced up – heavy clouds darkened the sky, blocking out all sunlight. I sagged. Sunlight would stop him, freeze him into a statue until twelve hours of darkness thawed him. But the clouds were too dark.

We could go through the doorway, I thought. He would follow, but we might have time to get to the stream in the human world before he could reach us. I hated taking the ring through the doorway again, but maybe that was better than letting Gronvald have it.

"To the doorway," I murmured to Maddy. I turned to Aleena and gestured with my head.

Aleena started to edge closer. As she moved, Gronvald moved with her, carefully keeping himself between Aleena and the stream.

While Gronvald stalked Aleena, Maddy and I quietly slipped over to the rock face towering above us. I flung a rock behind Gronvald, and when he spun around, Aleena dashed over to Maddy and me.

He spun back and growled at us, "Give me my ring. Give me my ring now, or DIE!"

Aleena just started at him, her chin tilted up, refusing.

Gronvald raised his hands to the top of the cliff and began muttering. I couldn't understand what he was saying – they were not words so much as sounds, rumbly and powerful, as if he was talking to the rocks themselves.

With a quick twist of his hand, a rock plummeted from the top of the rock face between us and the doorway. It smashed to the ground, shards breaking off and flying in all directions. We stepped back, gasping.

Gronvald grinned, and then muttered at the cliff

again. More rocks showered down around us. We pressed against the rock wall, using its slope to protect us from the rocks bouncing down from above.

"You'll kill us!" I said.

His grin widened. "That will make it so much easier to take the ring!" He pulled down another rock.

Aleena said, "After he kills us he'll be able to dig us out and get the ring – he's good with rocks."

Then Corvus called out, a powerful echoing, "CAAWWWW." He flew directly above us, along the face of the cliff, cawing wildly. What was he doing? Then I saw it. The top edge of the cliff was shifting loose.

Gronvald growled in anger and flung stones at Corvus.

Maddy cried, "Look out, Corvus!"

He cawed and turned, but before he could fly clear, he was hit by a rock and spun around. Then a boulder caught him, smashing him against the cliff wall. He fell past us, crushed.

He killed Corvus, I thought. *Corvus is dead!* I was stunned, but not too shocked to realized that Gronvald would kill us, too, if he could.

In a cawing mass, the crows attacked, led by the white-tipped crow. With a growl of anger, Gronvald lifted his hands towards the top of the cliff and pulled loose the front layer of rock.

Aleena and I both reached out to surround us with

magic, but Maddy grabbed our hands and slammed them into the rock wall. "Water," she panted. "Water travel, right now."

I could feel wet on the rock, a thin trickle of water falling down the cliff wall. Holding tight to Maddy's hand, I drew in magic, desperate to be faster than the rocks plunging down around us.

Maddy held tight to Aleena and me, and we shrank, becoming water. I could hear Gronvald crying, "Noooo!" in a desperate growl. As the top of the cliff face crashed down around us in a thundering roar, we flowed down the rocks and into the ground.

CHAPTER NINE

TREE SPIRIT

I AM WATER, I THOUGHT, AND THEN I DIDN'T think any more as I flowed through the earth, stretched thin through fissures, and floated through underground lakes. We travelled on and on and on. I couldn't imagine how I could stretch so thin or travel so far being water and ever become Josh again.

But then I was, as we rose through a thin stream of water into a rain forest.

"Corvus is dead!" Maddy burst out as soon as she could speak. "Gronvald killed him!" She sniffed. "He was warning us."

I hadn't liked Corvus, but I didn't want him dead. I closed my eyes for a moment and thanked him for protecting us.

"How did Gronvald find us?" I asked. "Will he be able to follow us here?"

Aleena nodded. "Oh, yes. He can smell the ring. He knew as soon as you took it out of Keeper's cave, and he will follow until he has it again."

"How could he smell it from so far away?" I asked.

"Magic," said Aleena with a shrug.

"Could I smell it?" I asked.

Aleena held out her hand, cradling the nexus ring.

"Yes," Maddy murmured, as I reached for it.

Then Aleena swallowed, and closed her hand over the ring. She slipped it onto her finger and held out her hand to me.

Maddy groaned in frustration and opened her mouth to say something, but I shook my head. *Not yet. She's not quite ready.*

I leaned down to Aleena's hand and sniffed. I smelled Aleena – moss and water, and the ring – an odd, earthy smell with depths I couldn't quite grasp. I felt that if I could, if I had enough magic, I could smell its life, where it had been, its entire history. But the smell was so faint. How could Gronvald follow that?

When I asked Aleena, she said, "It's his history, too. It was his ring for a long time."

I'm smelling Gronvald? I thought with horror. I gagged, and straightened.

"Will he be here soon?" Maddy asked.

"It'll take him a while. He travels through rock – through caves and tunnels and under mountains – but he'll get here."

Maddy shuddered, and I sighed.

We were in a dark rain forest, surrounded by massive trees. I gazed up and up, past trunks that reached forever, through branches searching for sunlight, finally spotting bits of grey-white sky through the mass of green.

As I peered upwards rain fell on my face. It dripped off the ends of evergreen branches, splashing down on enormous ferns and brilliant green moss coating rocks in thick blankets. More moss, in palest green, draped from dying branches in softly waving ghost-arms.

We followed a faint trail through a forest maze. I stared in wonder at enormous fallen trees, with saplings growing right out of their trunks. The ground was covered in a thick layer of forest debris, spongy underfoot and fragrant with cedar. I could smell green, and feel the forest growing.

Birds wove through the leaves, their songs filling the air. Magic flashed off their wings and fell like butterflies of light onto the plants below.

As I gazed around I wondered if it would be possible to paint this, to somehow capture the enormity and power of the trees, the greenness of the light, the radiance of it all when sunshine peered through the high branches.

We followed Aleena along the trail. As the forest darkened and the magic grew even deeper, Aleena came to a halt.

Ahead of us was the largest tree stump I'd ever seen. Instead of being red and crumbly, like the cedar stumps around us, it had hardened with age as if it was petrified. It was green with moss, and black in the deepest grooves.

Staring, I realized I was looking at a face carved deep into the wood, with large, dark eyes, high cheekbones and full lips. As I walked around it I saw a maze of fine cracks, with one deep crack running the full length of the face just beside the nose.

I stepped up to it and slowly ran my fingers over the wood. How old was this? It felt ancient, like old, deep magic. But wood rots – how could this not? And how was it made? Carved with an axe, perhaps? Shaped with knives? There were no tool marks, just wood grain and cracks and that face.

It was the most alive sculpture I'd ever seen. Not lifelike, a sculpture of a living thing, but alive, somehow, like the sculpture itself had life.

And then it opened its eyes.

I leapt back. Aleena started to laugh.

"What is it?" I asked Aleena in a hushed voice. I wasn't sure I wanted it to hear us talking about it.

Aleena replied just as softly. "Every species has a spirit. The tree spirit for the cedars is very old and large. Aspen are light and airy – each reflects the character of their tree."

She rested her hand on the base of the trunk. "Each sends out magic for the existence of their tree, even into the human world. The veil doesn't stop that – it doesn't need to. There is nothing humans can do to stop this. It exists. It simply exists. Every cedar, everywhere, in both worlds, is connected."

"Even if the trees are cut down?" I asked.

"The trees cut down are gone, but the tree spirit remains. This is ancient magic, older and deeper than any we use."

We squatted nearby to watch it. I wanted to sit closer, to be right beside that power, but at the same time I felt uneasy, as if it was watching me and not approving.

I studied the texture and the colours – moss green on the surface, black in the depths, with hints of red and gold as the light shifted. I reached out a hand, tracing the lines of its face in the air.

"Come closer," it said.

I almost leapt out of my shoes.

"Come closer. Touch me."

I shifted closer, reached out and gently traced a crack down its cheek.

It blinked slowly and I continued, entranced.

"Maddy," I said softly. "Come see this."

I took her hand and drew her closer. Aleena joined us, leaning in as we all slowly examined the face.

As I touched the wood, my hand reached through

it, as if it was no longer solid. Maddy and Aleena's hands penetrated through the face, too, as they softly stroked the wood.

Our eyes wide, we all breathed, "Oh!" Then we pulled our hands back. Except we couldn't. Something was holding us, more than holding us, slowly drawing us in. We braced our feet, fighting back, but it did no good. Slowly, smoothly, we were being drawn into the tree spirit.

We screamed, bellowed and kicked, but we couldn't stop it.

"Corvus," I cried, hoping that at least the crows could report back to Keeper. I heard no answering caw. Where were those crows when we needed them? Then I remembered. Corvus was dead.

I yelled as my arm was pulled deeper and deeper into the wood. Suddenly I couldn't cry out any more as my face and body were pulled into the trunk of the tree. Slowly it drew me in, through the wood deep into the centre of the tree. Our bodies were pulled into darkness, and then we were falling free, inside the trunk of the tree spirit.

The core of the tree was hollow, dark and oddly cozy. We untangled ourselves and each found room to sit, cushioned on soft, crumbly bark. A faint, richly red light made our skin glow darkly. By the dim light I could see tiny creatures in the bark, worms and ants and centipedes.

"Welcome," said a voice as warm as the light. It was neither male nor female, just rich and warm and deep.

"Why did you bring us here?" I asked.

"You cause too much damage. I will hold you here."

I gagged as my heart leapt up my throat. Hold us here? What did that mean? Keep us?

I looked all around. There were cracks in the wood, places where the wood was rotted and old. I was sure we could break out. I started to watch the centipedes; they would show us the weakest spots. As I studied the trunk, a lip of tree tissue began to grow around us, encircling us.

"What is this? What are you doing?" I said, fighting down panic.

"Growing a callus. That's what trees do – produce a callus tissue to cover the wound."

"We're not a wound," Maddy said. "We're people."

"You cause harm," the tree spirit said. "I can stop you. Therefore I must stop you." When it spoke we could feel the vibrations of its voice in the tree. "Now be quiet while I work."

We leapt up, but roots reached out and grabbed us, holding us in place as the callus rose around us. It grew into a little wall surrounding us, slowly, constantly rising.

"How do we do harm?" I asked, desperate to delay the tree spirit.

"She does, with the ring."

"I didn't mean any harm," Aleena said. "I just like to travel. That's all." I could hear the fear in her voice. We were all afraid.

"You are no different than Gronvald."

"No! I am not like him. I am not like him!"

"And what of the dead child-crow crushed in your hand? The snails, disturbed in their only home? The crows beaten by hail?"

"How do you know about that?" she asked, horrified. "Besides, they were just birds and snails – they don't count."

Maddy shook her head. "I think they all count," she said softly.

The tree spirit said, "I agree completely. They all count. Every living being counts." It sighed, and the wood groaned too. "I will not allow you to travel with the nexus ring. You may keep it, but you will keep it here."

"For how long?" I asked.

"For always."

Aleena gasped, and started to shake her head. "No, I can't stay here. I can't." I could hear panic building in her voice. "I need water – to swim, to play, to drink. I am a water woman – I cannot live here!"

She swallowed. "I'll give you the ring. You can keep it." She took the nexus ring off her finger and held it out in the palm of her hand.

"I cannot take it," the tree spirit said.

"I'll put it somewhere," said Aleena. "Just tell me where you want it."

The tree spirit laughed. I could feel the laughter shaking right to its roots. "I cannot keep it safe. I cannot protect it from any magic creature. I could not stop a centipede."

"But you stopped us," I said.

"Well, you are not a centipede. And I am not the keeper. I cannot keep the ring safe."

"We'll take it to Keeper," I said. "That's what we're trying to do. Well, Maddy and me." I let my voice fade out. It didn't seem right to tell on Aleena, to get out by sacrificing her.

But how could we get out? The callus continued to grow, surrounding us in tough, strong wood. I knew we had to act before it rose too high. Roots held us tight, holding us down, binding our arms to our sides. If we struggled, they tightened, squeezing us until we couldn't breathe.

I relaxed and the roots loosened their grip just a little. Barely moving, I eased a hand into my pocket and pulled out my firestone. It was easy to find the magic to lift out a thread of fire; the air was thick with magic. I pulled out a thread and fed a little magic into it. Golden light filled the inside of the tree.

"What are you doing?" asked the tree spirit, its voice suddenly rough.

"You will set us free," I said, "or I will burn you."

The tree spirit sighed. "Why do humans always need to destroy?" It sounded deeply sad. "I will burn, and so will you. Only the nexus ring will survive. Gronvald will smell it, past the odours of wood ash and burned flesh. He will find it, and he will cause even more damage than you have in your foolishness."

I let the fire go out.

Aleena huddled in a little bundle, smaller than I thought she could possibly fold herself, unable to look for any way to escape. It was as if the tree magic was overwhelming her water magic.

Desperate to find a way out, I drew in magic to calm myself. I could feel magic resonating here, even in the insects. I watched the bugs at work in the bark around us. A centipede walked up Maddy's leg, and she squealed.

"Watch it through your ring," I said.

She made a face, but I said, "Just try it."

Slowly she pulled her ring off her finger and looked at the centipede. She was immediately captivated, watching as it crossed her leg. It continued up and over the rim of callus growing around us.

"Josh, it's amazing," she said. "The long body glows as it moves. I can see every leg – I'm sure there must be more than a hundred. There's so much magic in this one little bug." She kept looking, examining every part of our prison, reaching out with a finger tip to touch whatever she was looking at. "I can see how the bugs all work together," she said, "eating the rotting wood, having babies, dying and being eaten."

Then she stopped. "Josh," she said in a soft voice.

"Hmmm?"

"Josh, I can see sap moving."

"But the tree's dead. It's just a trunk."

"No, it's not. Not really. And there's sap moving."

"Huh. That's weird."

"Josh, it moves like water, like a little stream of water." She stared at me, her eyes unblinking.

"Maddy!"

She shook her head and held a finger to her lips. "Just like a stream of water," she repeated softly.

My mind started to race. Sap – water – could we travel through sap and escape that way?

"Let me see," I said, and held out a hand for Maddy's ring. Moving slowly, I leaned into the roots over the lip of the callus, and peered through the ring into a crack in the trunk wall. Sap was slowly flowing up the tree. I touched it – it was sticky, too sticky. *It would be impossible*, I thought. We'd get stuck in it, or not be able to breathe. But when I relaxed into magic I could feel myself slipping into it.

When I nodded, Aleena stared. She shook her head. "I can't," she murmured.

"I can," I replied. "I'll take you. We have to get out now, before the callus grows higher."

She shook her head again, fearful. But when Maddy

and I took each other's hands and looked at her, she sighed and reached for us.

As we shrank, the roots tightened around us, and the tree groaned and creaked, but it couldn't hold us. I became water and moved into the sap, drawing Maddy and Aleena with me.

CHAPTER TEN

INTO THE EARTH

MOVING DOWN, AGAINST THE FLOW OF the sap, was almost impossible. The sap was a thick syrup, sticky and dense. I imagined being water, as tiny as possible, tightly attached to the other drops of Maddy and Aleena, and it became a little easier to move, to ease around and through the sap.

We moved deeper into the bark, where the sap was thinner, more like water. Still it tried to pull us upwards. But I was stronger, and slowly we flowed down the trunk of the tree while it groaned and shifted around us.

I wanted to travel through the ends of the roots into the soil near the surface, but I discovered that the cedar spirit's roots stretch far into the earth. We travelled deeper and deeper before reaching the tip of a root and then into the finest root hair. Finally, we slipped beyond the roots into damp soil.

As soon as we were free of the cedar tree, we were pulled into the earth, caught in a current of magic. We fought and tried to swim against it, but we didn't dare let go of one another. We were pulled deeper and deeper, down into the earth into old, thick magic.

Finally we slipped free of the earth and stopped in a long, narrow rock cavern. It was warm and dry and very dark.

As we reached air we began to grow, slowly, as the sap covering us contained us, clinging, stretching and finally breaking, leaving little pockets of sap all over us.

Maddy reached up to push her hair out of her face.

"No, don't touch," I cried, but I was too slow to stop her.

Her hands and her hair clung to each other, connected by sap. Maddy pulled her hands free, leaving her hair a tangled, sticky mess.

In all the growing and stretching, I didn't feel my normal size. I glanced at Maddy and Aleena and realized we were all the wrong sizes.

I was the tallest and the strongest. Maddy was the smallest as usual, but Aleena wasn't much taller than Maddy. She was oddly diminished here.

Light glowed off the walls, an eerie blue-green – the

rocks themselves were glowing. I could see patterns in the rocks, layers that shone more brightly than others. Our faces were lit by the pale light, making Maddy and Aleena look sick.

When I checked on them, I realized they really were sick. Maddy was struggling to breathe, her chest heaving in and out as she strained to draw in enough air. Aleena's skin was thin and dry, her eyes dull, her cheeks sunken. She looked gaunt and old.

I felt wonderful, strong and powerful. Magic flowed through me, filling me, making me part of the stone surrounding us. When I stood still, I could feel the earth breathing.

"We have to get out of here," gasped Aleena. "I am a water woman. Without water, I will die. We will both die. First me. Then Maddy." She touched Maddy's chest with a thin, dry hand.

I remembered how she'd described herself to me once, born of raindrops on moss. And I knew she spoke the truth, that she and Maddy would die here.

While Maddy and Aleena rested, I explored the cavern. It was large, long and narrow. The ceiling rose and fell, sometimes close enough for me to touch, sometimes rising high above us.

I searched for water, knowing we all needed to drink, and that Aleena especially needed water, but there was none.

There was a tunnel at each end of the cavern. One

sloped gently down: it was dark, and the magic thick.

The other curved up quickly, with steps cut into the steep slope. When I tried to climb the steps, I couldn't. My knees moved, but my feet wouldn't lift, as if they were glued to the ground. I could step away from the tunnel, but not into it. I tried sneaking at it, sideways and backwards, but whatever I tried, my knees could not lift my feet off the ground.

I walked back to Maddy and Aleena, hoping they were feeling better. If anything, they looked worse, Aleena slumped and thin, Maddy gasping.

I had to do something. I stepped into the lower tunnel and breathed in the thick magic. Using it, I sketched in the air, searching for an answer. Suddenly I felt an aliveness, a presence. I continued sketching until I had a name. Then I called out, "Earth, may we speak with you?"

Maddy and Aleena stared at me like I was nuts.

But the earth answered.

A low, husky voice resonated from the rocks all around us. "Human children and a water woman and the nexus ring. How very interesting." I heard a smile in the voice.

Maddy slipped her hand into mine. Aleena shivered, and drew closer to us.

"Maddy and Aleena are sick," I said. "They can't stay here."

"The nexus ring must go deeper," the voice

answered. "It is safer here than above, and safer below than here."

"We can't," I said. "Maddy and Aleena need to get to the surface."

The voice was silent. I waited. I was about to speak again when the voice said, "The water woman and the human girl? They are sick here?"

"Yes," I said. "I think your magic is too powerful for them."

"But not for you?"

"No," I said. "I love it."

The voice chuckled. "Yes. I can see that. You have – you have a great potential. To be what, I do not know. It will be interesting to see what you become." The voice sighed. "Very well. You shall take the ring as deep as you can, and they may walk to the surface."

Split up? Me, go deeper? Maddy and Aleena walk all the way back? I didn't know which I should be more upset about. Then Maddy bent over, struggling for air. She had to come first.

"It's too far for them to walk," I said. "It will take too long! Can't you send them back the way you brought us here?"

"No," the voice said, flatly. "You must take the ring deeper. You must take the ring to a safer place, where the shifting of rock and magma cannot bring it back to Gronvald. For every step you take deeper into the earth, they may take one step to the surface." The voice smiled. "This is more than fair, four feet up for two feet down."

I glanced at my feet and swallowed. That sounded pretty harsh to me. But when I looked at Maddy and Aleena I knew there was nothing else I could do. If I didn't start immediately, they wouldn't have the strength to walk out.

"Maddy," I said, "Just keep walking. Whatever happens, just keep walking."

"Aleena," I continued, "when you get to the surface, will you promise to take Maddy to Keeper?"

She shook her head, her eyes huge. "Not Keeper," she said, her voice dry and scratchy.

I remembered how much she feared him. "The otter-people?" I asked.

She nodded.

"Promise?" I demanded. "No matter what happens, no matter how sick you are, how close to death?"

She nodded again. "I promise." She slipped the nexus ring off her finger and handed it to me. "Thank you," she said, her voice rough.

She paused. Then she said in a louder voice, "Earth, what will happen to Josh?"

I knew how much that must have cost her, to speak past her fear and desperation to escape, her lips cracked, her throat parched.

When Maddy turned to her, puzzled, Aleena said, "Every one counts, right?"

Maddy smiled and took Aleena's hand. "Yes. Every one counts."

"The boy can withstand my magic," said the voice. "But will he come back to us?"

"That is up to him." That's all the voice would say.

I pulled the firestone out of my pocket. All the threads glowed, even in the stone, bright from the magic surrounding us. I tugged out one thread part way, leaving it half in and half out of the stone. It blazed like a torch, drawing magic out of the air.

I handed it to Maddy; the firestone continued to blaze. "I think it will get fainter as you go higher," I said.

Maddy smiled a little. "That'll mean we're going in the right direction."

I touched her chest, heaving as she struggled to breathe. "Your breathing should get easier, too. You'll need to help Aleena."

"I know," she said. "We'll be fine. And Josh?"

I looked down at her, blinking back tears.

"You'll be fine, too." She smiled. "I know I said earlier that I couldn't trust you with the nexus ring. But I was wrong. You can do this. I know you can."

I closed my eyes and sighed. "I will do it," I said. I took another breath. "I will do it. Now go."

She nodded and helped Aleena to her feet. Then she tucked herself under Aleena's arm, wrapped an arm around Aleena's waist, and turned towards the tunnel to the surface. When they got to the tunnel entrance, they stopped. I could see them trying to step forward, their knees straining, but their feet didn't leave the ground.

Maddy turned back to me. "We can take a step for every step you take."

"Oh yeah," I said. I closed my eyes, swallowed my fear, and walked to the other tunnel, sloping down even further into the earth. I took a step, and Maddy and Aleena lurched forward. I took another step down, and they took another up. But they couldn't get any kind of rhythm at that pace – they'd never make it to the surface before they died – so I squared my shoulders and strode down the tunnel.

CHAPTER ELEVEN

DEEP MAGIC

I CHECKED BEHIND ME OCCASIONALLY, SEEING A faint glow and a shadow as they moved. Eventually, even the flickering light vanished. I walked in darkness broken only by the slight luminescence in patches on the walls. I watched the colours shift as I walked deeper, from blue-green to bright blue, and then to a shining yellow.

It was painful to walk without knowing where Maddy and Aleena were. I longed to turn and run to them, but if they were to keep walking, I had to keep walking. I plunged on, down and down and down.

Finally I stopped to rest. I leaned against the rock wall of the tunnel, worrying about them. Without noticing, I started drawing on the rock – Maddy, always

Maddy – and soon I could sketch them as they walked, as if I could see them.

I sketched Maddy helping Aleena, staggering up the tunnel. Maddy was still struggling to breathe, but she was determined and immensely stubborn. Aleena was still overwhelmed and dehydrated, but she allowed Maddy to guide her. Then they came to a stop, unable to lift their feet. I realized I had to keep walking.

In a while I checked in again, sketching quietly on my pant leg as I walked. They were moving more quickly. Maddy's breathing had eased a bit, and Aleena was starting to stand on her own. I could tell by the light cast by the firestone that they were still deep in the earth. So I kept walking, the magic surrounding me growing thicker and thicker.

The next time I checked they'd found a large pool of water. After kneeling and touching a drop of water to her lips, Aleena stood and walked straight into the pool. She swam and floated and drank, letting the water soak in, reviving her. Maddy knelt and drank, washed her face and hands and arms, and took off her runners to soak her feet.

I rested while they did, and realized how thirsty I was, how much my feet hurt, how my stomach growled, how fear ate at me. I was glad when Maddy called to Aleena to continue. I could see Aleena testing to see if she could water travel, but she was still overpowered by the earth magic.

When she stood beside Maddy, Aleena was a little taller and looked much stronger. She and Maddy held hands and walked together, Maddy still taking deep, fast breaths, but moving more easily.

I stood, and continued down.

I walked forever, pushing everything else out of my mind, just walking, walking, walking. The air became so thick with magic it became harder and harder to move. I tried to distract myself by sketching Maddy and Aleena. They were walking side by side, no longer holding each other, and their firestone light was getting dim. They must be getting near the surface.

But as I sketched, I walked more and more slowly, and so did they. The magic was too thick – I couldn't push through it.

I heard the voice of the earth, for the first time since we'd left the cavern. "Let go of your art."

Let go of my art? No – I needed it to check on Maddy and Aleena. I loved it. I wanted it.

"You must let go of the art," said the voice again. I felt it almost more than I heard it, resonating in the rocks. "You can no longer use art to get to magic. Let go of the art. Be the magic." The voice was hypnotic.

I shook my head. *No, I wouldn't.* I kept walking, pushing, struggling to take each step. Soon I was panting and exhausted. It was like the magic was becoming sap and slowing me. With a quick sketch I saw that Maddy and Aleena could barely move, struggling with me to walk.

"You must become the magic," said the voice, soft and soothing.

I relaxed for a moment and slid right into it, right into that voice, right into the thickness of magic. In a panic I grabbed for something, anything to hold on to, but there was nothing. Nothing around me, no art, no drawing, no colour. Nothing at all.

But I could walk. I could stride down the tunnel, deeper and deeper into magic, letting it soak into me like water soaked into Aleena.

"This is deeper than art," said the voice "This is where art begins."

I walked for what felt like days, but I was no longer hungry or thirsty. *I am walking,* I thought. Then, later, *I am earth.*

I could feel it pulling me deeper and deeper until there was no me, no earth voice, just an immense power and quiet. In spite of the darkness all around me, it was filled with lightness.

I stopped and sat, watching the luminescence on the rock walls, a deep red shifting to purple, brightening into pink, and then yellow.

I knew that Maddy and Aleena were no longer inside the earth. But I had another task – what was it? I couldn't remember for the longest time. *I am earth,* I thought as I sat, but something was irritating me. I stared at my hands in my lap, feeling disconnected from them. Then I saw the nexus ring and remembered.

Clearly, without any doubt, I knew it didn't belong here. It would be safer here than with Aleena, but never truly safe. The earth moves, magma in the core becomes rock, and Gronvald can find anything in rock. The nexus ring had to be returned to Keeper, to be destroyed.

I didn't hesitate. I simply stood and started walking back up the tunnel. The magic didn't hold me any more, because I was the magic. It flowed with me, and I began walking again.

I followed the changing colours of luminescence back to the cavern, and then up the tunnel Maddy and Aleena had taken. I found their pool of water, and drank and soaked my feet and rested. Then I walked again, striding up and up.

As the luminescence shifted to gold, I stopped, sensing something. I listened carefully, and heard rocks smashing in the tunnel ahead of me. Slowly I crept forward. When I snuck around a curve I found a pile of rocks filling the tunnel more than halfway to the ceiling.

Through the gap I could see Gronvald, sweat gleaming as he cracked the rocks in the ceiling of the tunnel and pulled them down onto the growing heap.

My heart pounding, I thought about what I could do. There was no water here to travel through. I could walk back to the pool of water Aleena had bathed in, and see if it connected to a water flow. Or... I could still feel deep magic surrounding me. I drew it in, pulling it around myself like a cloak to hide in. Slowly, hardly daring to breathe, I started to climb the rock pile, letting the clatter of Gronvald's work hide the sound of rocks shifting under my feet.

As I drew nearer I could see Gronvald more clearly, his skin tinged by the gold luminescence. He was covered in rock dust, sweat dripping through it in trails down his body. He was panting and cursing as he worked, and he was very, very happy. Underneath the cursing I heard a rhythm and then a tune, as he crooned while he worked:

The nexus ring, the nexus ring,
Soon I shall have the nexus ring.
The boy shall die, they all can die,
And I shall have the nexus ring.

I swallowed. Groping in the shadows, I picked up a fist-sized rock, hefted it in my hand, and flung it up the tunnel. It bounced off the wall and crashed to the floor. Gronvald spun around and ran up the tunnel, searching for what had made the noise.

I climbed off the rock pile, careful not to make any sound or vibration. Pulling the deep magic tight around me, I gently slipped past Gronvald as he stood in the tunnel, turning around and around in confusion.

Then he stopped, sniffing. He'd smelled the nexus ring! With a cry he was after me, hands grasping, chasing me up the tunnel. I ran, feet pounding, letting the magic make me strong and fast.

We raced up the tunnel, Gronvald cursing and panting behind me. Soon I'd outrun him, but I didn't stop. I ran on and on, finally dashing out of the tunnel into daylight, high on a mountainside.

I stepped into sunlight and bent over, hands on my knees, struggling to catch my breath. When I straightened, I could see rows of mountain peaks stretching off into the clouds. I felt like I was looking across the top of the world.

Deep magic had dropped off me as I ran to the surface of the earth, like I was shedding a skin. I felt like Josh again, but a different Josh. There was nothing here I wanted to draw. I used to draw to become closer to things, to see more clearly, to become a part of them in a small way. Now all I had to do was breathe. I was a part of everything. I wasn't sure what art would mean to me now.

CHAPTER TWELVE

THE MAGIC BOY

I DIDN'T STAY LONG. I NEEDED TO GET BACK TO Castle Mountain to give the nexus ring to Keeper, and then to find Maddy.

I hiked down the mountain until I found a stream. Then I stepped into it, became water, and flowed down the mountain. I wasn't sure where I was or what mountain I was on, so I stayed in surface water, flowing down the mountain in a rapidly growing creek. Then I tumbled down a waterfall into a river.

I could see glaciers high on the mountains around me. I guessed I was in what was the Icefields Parkway in the human world, travelling north to the Arctic ocean. I turned and headed south, following the river towards its source in the glaciers. When the narrowing river turned up onto a mountain, I travelled down into the earth and found a water flow I could follow south. Soon I was back on the surface, floating downstream in the Bow River. I rested as the water carried me until I reached Castle Mountain. Then I found a creek tumbling into the river from the back side of Castle, and followed it up to the lake below Keeper's cave.

Keeper met me halfway up the mountain. I collapsed into his arms, leaning into him, letting him hold me up for just a moment. Then I pulled away. "Is Maddy here?" I asked.

He shook his head. "And clearly she is not with you," he said.

I sighed. "Aleena was supposed to take her to the otter-people. I'd hoped they would bring her here. I don't know where she is."

Keeper nodded, and bellowed across the mountainside. "Corvus, I have need of you."

I blinked. "Corvus is dead," I said.

Keeper just nodded again. "I know," he said, his voice gruff.

"Then – why did you call him?"

"There is always a Corvus," he said.

"But –"

Keeper smiled. "It is like a king, or a bus driver. There is always a Corvus. But I will miss old Corvus." He sighed, and bellowed again, "Corvus."

"What if he's not here?" I asked.

"He is not here."

"Then why are you shouting for him?"

Keeper smiled again. "All crows have ears. All crows have wings. They will tell Corvus I have need of him. While we wait, let me look at you."

He placed his huge hands on my shoulders and stared down at me. Then he nodded his approval. "Yes," he said, sighing deeply. "As I thought. You have much magic, Josh. Do you have the nexus ring?"

"Yes," I said, fumbling in my pocket for it. "I put it away, hoping Gronvald wouldn't smell it as easily if it wasn't on my finger." I pulled it out and handed it to Keeper.

He reached for it, his hand closing over it. "You have made me very proud, Josh. I have seen something in you, something – I am not sure what. But I hoped. Now I see that I was right."

"What do you mean?" I asked, embarrassed and confused.

He smiled. "I see magic in you, Josh. My magic boy."

My breath caught in my throat. Magic boy? What was that? Then I remembered the nexus ring, and knew we had to stay focused.

"You need to destroy the nexus ring," I said. "It can't ever damage the veil again."

He nodded. "Yes. We will destroy it. Come," he said, and strode up to his cave. I scrambled after him, struggling to keep up now that deep magic wasn't propelling me.

Keeper ducked his head as he entered his cave, picked up a torch and blew gently to light it. Instead of walking deep into the cave to the slab where he kept the rings, Keeper turned in to his workshop and walked up to a blacksmith's anvil, a massive block of iron. He wiped it clean with one hand, and laid the ring on it.

He stepped over to his tools, ran his hand over them and chose a huge hammer, long handled with a heavy head. He walked back to the anvil, swung the hammer high over his head, and smashed it down on the ring. The anvil reverberated in a great gong that echoed up the cave.

I watched with a tight smile as he smashed the hammer down again and again.

"The ring is much more dangerous than I thought," Keeper said between blows. "It can not be allowed to exist."

The ring was soon smashed to a fine powder. I could smell it – rock and wildness and ancient secrets, and somehow I could smell Gronvald and Aleena and Maddy and even me.

While I was shocked to see it smashed to dust, there was something right about this. For the first time since I'd seen the gash in the veil through Maddy's ring, I felt good. *At least I've accomplished this*, I thought. But I felt no joy. Not without Maddy.

Keeper carefully brushed the dust of the crushed ring onto a square of red cloth. The dark green dust scattered across it, still gleaming. "We will give it to the wind," he said, as he folded the cloth over the nexus dust.

When we stepped back into the main part of the cave, the white-tipped crow was waiting for us.

"Corvus," said Keeper, dipping his head in respect.

"Crawww," said the white-tipped crow, bowing his head in return.

"Where is the human child Maddy?" asked Keeper.

I watched in astonishment as new-Corvus began to strut across the floor, cawing and muttering as he told his story. His caws varied, sometimes loud and harsh, sometimes slow and soft, sometimes shifting to quiet mutterings that sounded almost human.

Keeper listened, and started to interpret for me. "Corvus says, they lost track of you whenever you water-travelled with that witch, Aleena." He cleared his throat. "That is not what I call her. That is the term Corvus uses."

I nodded, trying not to smile.

"Crows searched, found, lost again, searched again. Then for a long time they could not find any of you." Keeper paused, and Corvus spoke again.

I listened to him cawing, my whole body tense, wanting them to get on with it, to tell me where Maddy was.

Corvus stopped, and Keeper turned to me to interpret again.

"Finally they spotted Aleena and Maddy, with the otter-people Greyfur and Eneirda."

My body sagged in relief. I slumped to the floor to listen to the rest of the story.

"They are bringing her by boat. Their infernal magical boats, says Corvus." Keeper and I grinned at each other. Then Keeper cleared his throat and continued, trying to look serious. "At least the boat is easier to follow than water travel. They will be here soon."

I jumped up. "Thank you, Corvus," I said. I bowed my head in thanks.

He bobbed his head, turned and strutted out of the cave, caws echoing behind him.

Keeper and I followed. We stood in front of Keeper's cave and stared down to the lake below. No Maddy, not yet.

A small crow flew up to me and landed on my head. I shook him off, yawned, and stretched out my arms, finally starting to relax. Suddenly I was a coat rack for crows, as they swarmed around me, settling on my arms.

"What are they doing?" I squeaked.

Keeper laughed and called out to Corvus. "Perhaps they could sit on the ground nearby."

Corvus barked out a few harsh caws, and the crows lifted off my arms and settled on the ground around me. They strutted and preened their feathers, softly muttering, but always nearby. When I walked, they followed, always maintaining a circle around me.

"What is this?" I asked.

Keeper chuckled. "They like your magic. They consider themselves an honour guard for the magic boy."

I choked back a laugh. "Corvus," I said, as respectfully as I could. "The crows do me a great honour. I thank you. I think it would be easier for me and safer for the crows if they weren't in front of me when I walk. I don't want to hurt anyone."

Corvus cawed to me, and then muttered to the crows. After that they gathered behind me, or flew nearby. If they needed to be really noisy, they'd move away to a tall tree where they could talk and fuss all they liked, but one always stayed near me.

Finally, I spotted the boat, a round bark boat just large enough to fit whoever needed to ride in it. Maddy and the otter-people had come up the creek I'd used, up from the Bow River to the lake behind Castle Mountain. Joy filled me as I watched Eneirda paddling, Maddy safe and happy in the front of the boat.

Keeper and I started hiking down the mountain to meet them. The crows flew, circling and cawing in a festive mass.

The boat pulled up to the shore where the path reached the lake, and Maddy, Eneirda and Greyfur stepped out. Greyfur pulled the boat safely on to shore, while Eneirda laid the paddles back in the boat for their return journey.

When Maddy saw me, she cried out a greeting and flew up the mountainside. "Josh, Josh!" she yelled. "You did it. I knew you could do it!"

Then my heart stopped as I heard a roar from below me. I stared down to see Gronvald leaping out of the wall of the mountain. I couldn't see where he'd come from – it must have been from a cave or crevice in the cliff face.

He leapt for Maddy, bellowing "I want my ring!" His voice echoed back and forth against the mountains, sounding like dozens of trolls surrounding us.

He hurtled down the mountain towards her, panting and furious. As he raced past, below me on the mountainside, I flung myself off the cliff above him, toppling him before he could reach Maddy. We rolled and bounced down a scree slope, loose rock sliding under us, dumping us down towards the lake. I could hear shouts from behind and above as the others scrambled to reach us.

We flipped over each other, bouncing off rocks, and then skidded to a stop against the side of a huge boulder. Gronvald was on top, pinning me to the ground. Rocks dug into me from below. I struggled and tried to throw him off, but Gronvald was bigger and heavier and much meaner. He grabbed my head, ready to smack it against the rock.

Then Keeper bellowed, "Gronvald!", his voice filling the valley. He stood high above us, his arms outstretched, dark against the mountainside. "Gronvald, I give you your ring," he said, pulling the red cloth out of his pocket and tossing it high into the air. The nexus dust floated free, sparkling darkly as the wind caught it. The red cloth drifted slowly to the surface of the lake.

The scent bloomed on the wind, rushing past us as the wind grabbed it and swirled it around the valley. Gronvald's voice cried out a pain-filled "Noooo!" as he inhaled the scent.

He jumped off me and grabbed at the nexus dust carried on the wind. He stood at the edge of the shadows reaching for the dust, hand opening and closing, not able to step into the sunlight, not able to get any closer. He moaned in pain as he watched the nexus dust drift away towards the mountain peaks. His face crumpled; he howled in rage and betrayal.

"I will never forgive this!" he screamed. "I – Will – Never – Forgive!" Then he slipped into a crevice in the rocks and disappeared.

Maddy raced across the mountainside to me, and helped me clean off the dirt and blood from my tumble down the mountain.

"I knew you could do it," she said quietly, as she slipped her hand into mine.

"Did Aleena come with you?" I asked.

"Not likely!" said Maddy. "But she did make sure I

was safe with the otter-people."

"Was she okay about losing the nexus ring?"

"No, but she was happy to be alive. And maybe secretly glad not to have it. If she had it, she'd have to choose – should I use it or not? I think she saw it as a big test she was sure to fail."

I nodded. We stood with our arms around each other as Keeper joined us.

Maddy asked him, "Will Gronvald leave us alone now?"

"Yes. There is no ring for him to fight for. But there are still tears he can use. And he will."

"They'll heal, won't they?" I asked.

"Yes, they will heal," Keeper said. He sighed as he turned away, and he didn't say how long it would take.

"I'm so sorry, Keeper," I said.

He looked down at me. "I am no longer Keeper. I was Keeper of the nexus ring. Now there is no nexus ring. I am no longer Keeper."

He smiled gently at us as we stared at him in shock. Then he said, "The names of giants change. Change is good."

"You'll always be Keeper to us," said Maddy, as she slid her small hand into his.

Keeper smiled and patted her hand.

Greyfur and Eneirda joined us.

"You take big risks, *tss*," Greyfur said to Keeper.

Keeper nodded. "When you are as big as I am, how

can you take small risks?"

Greyfur shook his head. "To risk all, by trusting in *humans?*"

"Not *humans*," Keeper said. "Maddy, who belongs in our world like no human ever has, and Josh, my magic boy."

"*Ssst!* Is that what you have been creating, a magic boy?"

Keeper just smiled and rested a hand on my shoulder. "It is time for you to go home," he said. He grabbed our backpacks from inside the cave entrance. I checked for my sketchpad, and pulled on my ball cap.

Keeper, Eneirda and Greyfur walked with us, and the crows flew, some scouting ahead, others circling around us, keeping guard. The otter-people stayed on the far side of Maddy, glancing at me occasionally, as if they were trying to figure out what I had become.

When we reached the Castle Mountain Lookout trail, I opened the doorway. Then Keeper tried to teach me how to cross time so we could get back to just before our parents arrived.

"Just slip along the veil," he said, "until you get to the time you need."

I stepped into the doorway, not sure I could do it. But when I focused, I could feel the veil, light and smooth, and as I thought about time shifting it moved past me, slowly at first, and then faster and faster.

Keeper yanked me back. "Whoa!" he said, his voice

full of laughter. "You can do this too easily, my magic boy. You will need to learn control. I will do it this time."

I stood with him in the doorway, and felt him shift the veil to just after Maddy and I had first crossed into the magic world.

"You don't want to meet yourselves," he said.

After hugs from Keeper, finger touches from Greyfur and Eneirda, and a chorus of caws from the crows, Maddy and I stepped into the doorway.

We walked through the mist into the human world, to hear Mom and Dad calling for us.

"Here," I said, following their voices.

"There you are," Dad said. "Where have you been?"

"We were sitting over there," I said, pointing towards a viewpoint just out of sight, "while we ate our sandwiches. We're still hungry. Do you have any more food?"

Dad laughed. "Of course we have more food."

"Didn't you hear us calling?" Mom asked.

"No, sorry," Maddy said. Then she laughed softly. "I guess we were off in another world."

We grinned at each other as Dad rummaged in his backpack, and crows circled overhead.

ACKNOWLEDGMENTS

WITH DEEP THANKS TO Barbara Sapergia, who convinced me the first draft didn't work, which led, eventually, to a better story.

And more thanks to Laura Peetoom, my editor, and the staff at Coteau Books for the wonderful work they do.

Photograph by Mark Harding

ABOUT THE AUTHOR

MAUREEN BUSH has published two other novels, including the first in this series, *The Nexus Ring*; and *Feather Brain*. Her books have been short-listed for numerous awards including the Silver Birch and the Saskatchewan Diamond Willow. Maureen has a post-graduate certificate of creative writing from Humber College. She also obtained a bachelor's degree in history and a masters in environmental design (environmental science), both from the University of Calgary.

Born in Edmonton, Maureen Bush now lives in Calgary with her husband and two daughters.

Printed and bound in Canada by Friesens

Mixed Sources

Cert no. SW-COC-001271
© 1996 FSC